MARS iN CARNAGE

William Paul Lazarus

WolfSinger Publications ❨ Brackettville, TX

BOOK ONE:

FiRST
F(L)iGHT

CHAPTER 1

Sitting in his office chair, where he had been for most of the previous two days, Lt. Col. John Hathaway wearily leaned forward and tapped the control to play the tape again. He put his arm over his bleary eyes and tried to focus as the familiar words started. He didn't know how many times he had listened to them, but he kept hoping to uncover some clue in Commander Aadya "Kate" Khatun's last transmission. Her communication from Mars had ended 40 hours prior, with her final few words arriving in Mission Control 14 minutes after she spoke them.

Kate was talking, almost in a whisper, as if trying to conceal her presence inside the small capsule nicknamed MOM that landed on Mars hours earlier with her and her partner Lt. Commander Hamza "Arti" Artsruni. The tape began with: "I can see Arti. He must be lying maybe 15 meters away from MOM. He isn't moving. He was going to the small cave when he fell. I didn't see anything hit him. He just fell face first."

Small, quick breaths. "I really should go out there. I feel very guilty just watching."

Silence for six seconds.

"What was that?" Noises, including a small bang. "Something smashed into the ground behind the module. I don't want to leave MOM, but I may have to. She's listing. Whatever hit the ground caused a small crater. The back end is tilted at a forty-five-degree angle. Wait a minute." A pause." "The closed-circuit monitor is showing a lot of dots. I see flashes. MOM is rocking. I can see stones flying in the air and lots of dust."

Another pause.

"The aliens must be shooting at MOM. I can't stay here. I can't tell how many ships are firing. They are very inaccurate. That's not a bad thing. They are moving rapidly."

Pause. More panting.

"It's hard to sit here. The computer has shut down. I hope you can hear this. At least the monitor is allowing me to see what's going on outside."

Pause.

"Lots of noise. I can see at least a dozen planes. One just swooped past MOM. I wish I had an anti-aircraft gun."

Pause.

"I am not afraid of dying here. I am just not fond of the idea of being captured by aliens. If one of them tries to grab me, I'll remove my helmet and walk outside. I won't last long. I know that."

Pause.

"It's odd to think of Arti being dead. From the looks of it, the back of his helmet has been crushed. He thought we'd be better off if we split up. I disagreed, but he wasn't thinking straight. The long flight can really warp the brain. We did everything to stay active, but he seemed to be having a lot of trouble. I guess it doesn't matter now. No place is really safe. Sure hate to think we flew millions of miles just to meet some hostile aliens. Aren't they supposed to say, 'Take me to your leader?' These guys never got the memo."

Pause.

Rapid breathing.

"So far, the readings on the radar screen show our mother ship is still in orbit. They haven't tried to take it out yet. All their focus seems to be on the ground."

Why? Hathaway thought, not for the first time. The Odin would be an easy target. Unmanned and lacking any weapons. Maybe the aliens could tell that and were focusing on an enemy they could see. What kind of equipment did they have that allowed them to identify life forms? Heat detectors? Carbon dioxide detectors?

"The dots are coming closer. I can clearly see it's a small kind of airship with a rotator, like a helicopter, except much faster and more maneuverable. Reminds me of a wasp. Man, I'd love to fly one of them. I can't see any rear exhaust. I don't know what kind of propulsion system the planes have. They really zip around."

Pause.

"One has landed." Gasp. "It just dropped down easily, like a Harrier. But faster. Not much dust. The rotor has stopped. I don't see a door. There it is. Stairs dropped down from under the cockpit. I don't see anyone yet. Wait. Someone is walking down. Bipedal. Two arms. Very human like. Helmet. Very thin. The front of the helmet is reflective. Looks like he's wearing some kind of dark uniform. I don't see any insignia. He is standing next to Arti. Don't do that!

He turned Arti over with his foot. That's awful. He's unhooking Arti's helmet. It's off. He's looking at Arti. I don't see any communication equipment, like a radio or anything. I can't tell if he's reporting anything. Oh, no! He's looking at MOM. He's walking this way! He doesn't seem to have a weapon. Radiation readings just shot up. Maybe that will stop him."

Pause.

"I'm going back into storage and shutting the door!"

That was it. The tape ended. All video from Mars had ceased long before the audio conked out. The computers in Mission Control showed only blank screens and had from shortly after the two astronauts toasted each other during their arrival celebration. Kate's audio also ended and then resumed after a 12 minute 45 second delay, but video was no longer being recieved.

Hathaway rubbed his forehead. Was he missing something? Kate was in the module, which had begun to tilt because of damage to the supporting ground. She had seen lots of aircraft and shelling. One alien plane had landed. The occupant had stepped out. He resembled a human and wore a helmet. Did that mean he could not survive in the weak Martian atmosphere? He checked Arti and then moved toward the module.

Thoughts raced through Hathaway's mind. Had Kate survived? Had she been captured? The module had no weapons, but the interior door could be sealed shut. She would have enough food and oxygen for a few days. How long would the aliens stay? Would they have any reason to stick around if they thought both the module and ship were empty? They had no base there. No obvious presence. The robotic Rovers had traveled around the planet and detected no signs of life nor had any alien interfered with their roaming.

His secretary Patricia Wei came in with more coffee. She had a sympathetic look on her face. Secretaries must have training in that, Hathaway thought idly. His secretary in the Pentagon wore the same wry expression when a U.S. jet vanished over the Pacific Ocean. Hathaway looked at the cup. All he could see was an image of Kate in the rising steam.

Unable to think of anything else to do, he again dialed Boeing engineer Hal Worthington in Huntsville to check on the status of the backup rocket. The engineer didn't take the call. Hathaway didn't get upset. The poor man was trying to rush construction and had to be a bit annoyed by the steady stream of calls, like a child asking, 'are we there yet?'. Even if by some miracle the rocket could be ready in a month, they couldn't reach Mars for an additional four to five months. Plus, who would want to go anyway? The aliens could still be within distance to attack. A space trip to probable death hardly seemed appealing. Mission Control could arm the astronauts, but the aliens appeared to possess superior technology.

Reached via an internet call, Hathaway's boss, PAL Industries owner Pohl Andre Laarson, listened to the tape. Hathaway had waited to contact Laarson, who funded the initial Martian exploration. Once the crew left Earth, Laarson had stayed away, just getting occasional updates, so he didn't know what had happened on Mars; neither did the public. However, Hathaway reasoned, he couldn't wait any longer. The media would find out soon enough anyway, and Hathaway didn't want Laarson informed that way.

After listening to Hathaway's report, Laarson seemed unconcerned. Hathaway hadn't expected a strong reaction, as he well knew, Norwegians could be very stoic. Laarson nodded once or twice, as though enjoying a radio opera. His smile remained. *Maybe,* Hathaway thought, *he doesn't understand the depth of the crisis.* So, he played the tape for a second time.

"I do not see why we cannot try again," Laarson finally said, adding one of the Norwegian idioms he was so fond of: "*Storm i et vannglass.*"

"It's not that simple. It's not a storm in a glass of water," Hathaway answered. "I can see one very dangerous reason for never going to Mars again." He paused before adding a Norwegian phrase he had learned: "*bedre føre va.*"

Laarson laughed. "You are a quick study, but I do not believe in taking precautions," he said. "Next time, we'll go armed with mortars and long-range missiles. We will blast them from the sky."

"With all due respect," Hathaway said, "it's a suicide mission. Who will man the guns?"

"I can see it," Laarson said. "Like your Old West. Have you forgotten?"

Hathaway ignored the comment. Astronauts were brave; but they definitely weren't stupid. The science fiction pap fed to movie-goers for years had created illusions of what miracles humans could perform when confronted with hostile enemies. Millions of miles from home, isolated, however, no one could survive long with only the available equipment to rely on, especially with well-armed aliens lurking in the neighborhood.

He didn't interrupt Laarson; the man was a self-made trillionaire, only 25, and no one was going to silence him. Eventually, Hathaway claimed a bogus call from Mission Control and closed the session.

Exhausted, Hathaway fell asleep in his office. He awoke, groggy and disoriented to his phone ringing. His wife was on the line. Checking the time, he saw he had only slept for two hours. He sipped cold coffee while assuring his wife he was all right.

Stop trying to handle this alone, Eva suggested. Hathaway agreed. She was right; everyone had a stake in what happened, especially when the news of aliens attacking the astronauts was released. Hathaway drew up a short list of people to plan strategies; Laarson wasn't on it. He was busy reveling in the extensive media coverage while, at the same time, mourning the brave astronauts, whom he compared to the Norwegian soldiers of World War II and their battles against the overwhelming forces of Russia and Nazi Germany

Wei contacted the chosen participants. Hathaway wanted to keep the session small and limit exposure. As a result, all his choices were already at Cape Canaveral. No one had to fly there and risk alerting the media. After a shower and some clean clothes, Hathaway convened a meeting. By then, evening was settling over the Cape, with long shadows and concordant dark thoughts. One by one, the participants trooped into the conference room down the hall from Hathaway's office: the oldest ranking astronaut, Jack Kelly; NASA assistant director, Heloise Simpson; Hathaway's assistant Miguel Consuelo; White House senior aide Hereford G. Collins; and Dr. Ellie Dennis, NASA consultant on alien life.

Greeting each other with somber looks and dour expressions, they entered the conference room. They sat around the large table, which was ebony and seemed to reflect their moods. On the wall, the portraits of past astronauts smiled down at them. The screen behind Hathaway was blank. If all systems had been working, cameras on Mars would have been broadcasting images of the astronauts', but video still had not returned.

Wei served coffee.

Hathaway did not welcome them. Instead, after briefly reviewing the situation, he explained the purpose of the gathering. Everyone nodded. From their expressions and haggard appearances, Hathaway could tell they also had gotten little rest.

"Any update?" Collins asked.

"None."

"I haven't given up hope," Kelly said. "Kate can be really resourceful."

"I am sure you are right," Simpson said. She must have realized her enthusiasm rang false because she immediately quieted.

They all did, for a very long time.

Finally, Hathaway spoke. "Now what?" he asked.

No one answered. He slumped in his chair. Exhausted, he stared at the ceiling. He took out his earpiece and placed it on the desk. The others watched him. It seemed to signal resignation. He knew that. He just couldn't bear the silence anymore. How did they ever reach this point? With the others lost in their own thoughts, Hathaway watched the scenario play out from the beginning on the shadowy ceiling.

CHAPTER 2

Facing a room full of reporters and guests inside the cavernous Kennedy Space Center Apollo/Saturn V Center, Commander Aadya Khatun felt insignificant. A raised platform gave her some height, but the wooden podium masked much of her body, leaving only her head and shoulders visible. Yet, she remained resolute, looking out at the massive audience in attendance and with millions more watching on television. Other dignitaries who could not attend the media conference appeared as rows of heads on the electronic screens encircling the room. The faces kept changing as people signed in. Nothing seemed to faze Khatun, who maintained a strong, composed stare. Hathaway was very proud of her.

Deliberately dressed in a gray suit to contrast with the blue-uniformed astronauts, Hathaway had picked her from among the team of astronauts training at Cape Canaveral in Florida to become one of the first two people to land on Mars. He listened as she introduced herself and gave a little of her background: born in Bangladesh, undergraduate degree from Embry-Riddle Aeronautical University, a doctorate in planetary geology from Brown University, and one of only two women currently in the NASA astronaut training program. None of that happened by chance. Khatun—Kate to her friends—planned every step well in advance, a trait Hathaway admired.

He glanced to the side. His assistant Consuelo had discretely removed the two empty chairs reserved for Kate's parents. She never said a word about their lack of support. Hathaway had hoped the ship's sponsor, PAL Industries, could convince them to come to the launch. Even Laarson had failed. In his own discussions with the parents, Hathaway listened politely as Kate's father, Achintya, stressed that, while his daughter certainly had gone far, in his culture, women did not aspire to be astronauts. Nor did they climb into a rocket ship with a single man to be together for at least eight months.

Achintya spoke in clean, clipped words that masked the anger simmering beneath the surface. "Culturally," the older man had said, "the eldest son should represent the family in such an adventure." Hathaway decided not to mention Kate's brother, Arup, was useless and lived in his parents' home with a wife, two children and no job. Hathaway just nodded at Achintya's claims and suggested the family appreciate the unique opportunity for a woman. Clearly, they did not.

Listening now to Kate's recitation, hearing her amplified words echoing around the spacious room and through the multiple microphones attached to the podium, Hathaway could not hide his pleasure at her performance. With her long hair tied back in a severe bun to emphasize her serious intent, Kate seemed the epitome of earnest sincerity. Moreover, she thanked her parents and did not acknowledge their absence. To Hathaway, Kate's carefully worded comments reinforced his reasons for selecting her: she was discreet, tactful and yet self-motivated enough to override the anti-female prejudice in her family, her native country and even at a major university where few women entered her chosen field.

That fierce will gave a hard edge to her words, underlining her commitment to the mission. She also lowered her register to give her voice a more masculine tone, an effort that amused Hathaway.

The hundreds of reporters sitting on wooden chairs inside the visitors' center recorded her comments amid the array of TV cameras. The adjacent cafeteria had been turned into a catering center for the media, many of whom seemed to be balancing paper plates on their glossy media kits as they entered computerized notes and comments into their various devices. A few reporters continued grazing while Kate talked, looking back now and then to be sure she was still there before harvesting more food.

The sounds of their foraging merged with the endless tapping of computer keys and the murmur of voices to generate a steady hum in the room, akin to the constant static from the explosion that created the universe. Only the scraping of chairs against the hard flooring occasionally interrupted the underlying noise.

As the PAL mission director, Hathaway carefully watched the sprawling scene, noting reactions of the VIPs seated on the right side. They were talking among themselves with an occasional glance at the dais. The Florida governor had moved to a small corner with several aides. Hathaway saw the NASA director had moved next to one of the two Florida senators, who had gleaned a large quantity of jumbo shrimp. The director was carefully explaining something while the senator chomped away with studied disinterest. At least the senator's secretary was dutifully recording the comments.

Among the rows of spectators, Hathaway also spotted at least three celebrities, nodding and waving to invisible fans while surrounded by a coterie of burly bodyguards. Their presence was not a surprise. All three—two women and a man—had previously purchased rides on the SpaceX, Blue Origin or Virgin Galactic tourist shuttles for brief journeys to the edge of space and back.

Behind all of them, the huge Saturn V rocket of another era stretched back more than 100 meters, seemingly pointing toward the stage and the newest astronauts.

"I don't think about the danger," Kate said in flawless English in answer to a question. Her image was displayed on the huge screen hanging behind her. There, she seemed large enough to handle such a gathering. "I am honored to be chosen for such a mission," she continued, adding she was proud to serve as a role model for women everywhere. She maintained a steady tone without a hint of a nervous quaver or an accent. Standing about 10 feet to her left, Hathaway tried to stay in character as the impervious leader of this privately funded mission but had trouble suppressing his smile at her composure.

After a few more questions, Hathaway moved to stand next to Kate. He could see the slight evidence of sweat on her forehead, the only hint of inner turmoil. Despite practice sessions, neither of the astronauts were really prepared to face such an audience. However, Kate seemed to be a natural. Stepping back, she acknowledged him with a slight smile. He nodded to reassure her.

"Thank you, Kate," he said.

Speaking into the microphone and hearing his words echo a second or so behind his actual voice, Hathaway introduced the second astronaut: Lt. Commander Hamza Artsruni, a young man from Turkey. Nicknamed Arti, he strode across the wooden flooring and stood rigidly, almost at attention. Resembling a guard, he had been waiting on the back of the stage, hands by his side, head erect, staring straight ahead. Kate took his place in the rear of the stage, but in a more relaxed pose, although her dark eyes continued to survey the crowd as if on alert for danger.

The crowd applauded Arti, led by his father and mother who

gave him a two-person standing ovation from their seats. Arti seemed slightly embarrassed by their efforts, which continued for several seconds after the others had ceased. He finally waved at them to be seated. His mother perched on the edge of her chair and gazed at him with devout fervor.

Dressed in a traditional jumpsuit ironed to rigid perfection, Arti also began with a brief outline of his life in Turkey, his decision to become a geologist, graduation from Dartmouth with a doctorate in geology and environmental science, completion of pilot training before being "overwhelmed" by the opportunity presented him to be a member of the first Martian expedition.

Hathaway kept a close eye on him. In a couple of early training sessions, Arti had shown a quick temper, especially when frustrated by some exercise. Hathaway doubted any question would set him off, but that character flaw that almost got him removed from mission consideration. The only reason it didn't was Kate had been disciplined in college for bopping some overeager fellow student with a textbook. Apparently, he got too close for comfort. Since Hathaway was willing to forgive Kate's youthful transgression, he felt obligated to ignore Arti's outburst. Laarson pushed for Arti, too. He never said why, but Hathaway was happy to acquiesce to his boss' urging.

Besides, Arti was incredibly smart, inventive, self-motivated and confident. Athletic, he was in superb physical condition, handling that facet of training with ease and seeming a perfect match for Kate, who also trained rigorously. The two got along very well after being selected, a necessity for a trip that would keep them in close quarters for about four months there and four months back.

Hathaway asked for questions. A reporter in front raised his hand. A runner quickly brought him a microphone. "Leon Glenn, UPI," the man said. "I would like to address Lt. Commander Artsruni." The young man tightened his lips in response, as if steeling himself. The room quieted, except for the senator loudly depleting international shrimp supplies and the whirr of cameras. "As a Turk…" Glenn began.

Arti interrupted him immediately. "I am Armenian," he said with extra stress and an obvious accent. Hathaway immediately turned to look at the astronaut. He could see Arti's dark eyes flash.

"As an Armenian," Glenn corrected himself. "Do you…"

"It's important to emphasize that I am Armenian," Arti interrupted again, addressing the entire audience. Everyone stared at him. Even the senator stopped chewing. Artsruni glanced sideways at Hathaway, who gave a slight shake of his head. Arti saw the gesture, but did not stop.

"Arti," Hathaway cautioned under his breath.

Arti ignored him. "Our land was taken from us," he said forcefully. "More than a century ago, my people were killed and marginalized. Still, we are a proud people. My status as one of two Martian astronauts testifies to the strength and resilience of the Armenian people."

Glenn gave a slight bow of apology. "I only meant to ask if you see yourself as a role model for a part of the world that is often overlooked," he continued.

Arti paused. "Overlooked? By who?" He almost spat the words. "My people once ruled an empire before this continent housed nothing more than a few natives. I am proud of my heritage. How others see me is their business," he replied as if lecturing.

Glenn shrugged, sat down and relinquished the microphone. Arti's parents erupted in applause. His father clenched a fist and shook it with pride in the general direction of the cafeteria.

Hathaway quickly patted Arti's left hand, which was tightly gripping the side of the podium. "Are there any more questions?" he asked as Arti calmed himself.

"Al Griffin, Reuters," a middle-aged man in a suit said, taking the hand-held microphone from the runner. "Commander, I was wondering about the feasibility of a man and woman traveling together on such a long journey. Or maybe that should be addressed to Col. Hathaway."

Arti glanced at Hathaway, who moved to the microphone. This was exactly why he hated press conferences and the media. All the "gotcha" questions. The media didn't want information; the reporters just wanted to prove their own intelligence.

Hathaway forced a smile. "I understand your concern," he said. "This is an issue that weighed into the decision of which astronauts to send. PAL Industries wanted two people to pioneer our exploration of Mars. We knew strength would be required to handle the equipment necessary to bore into the surface. However, we were reluctant to choose only men. Few women have ever been astronauts; none went to the Moon. Two died going into space—Judith Resnick and Christa McAuliffe. However, we realized two women alone could not easily employ the equipment. On the other hand, we wanted a woman to demonstrate a woman could be as capable as a man on such an important and dangerous mission."

He paused. "The pairing worked for God, didn't it?" he added. That drew a nice laugh.

Griffin didn't relinquish the mic. "Are you suggesting they are supposed to begin populating Mars?" he asked. "Is that why both come from similar areas?"

Hathaway shook his head. "Their nationality is immaterial," he said. "For some reason, Americans think they have the monopoly on adventurous people who will bravely go where no man has gone before, to quote the movies. They don't. We chose the best candidates. These two stood out among the astronauts in training. They just happened to not be American. Besides, I am American and am commanding this exploration. We are in Florida, on American soil, in an American facility."

"It's rented," someone scoffed.

Waving Arti away from the front of the podium, Hathaway waited a moment before responding. Everyone heard the comment; he could not let it pass. Besides, he had been expecting that kind of scorn. After all, Pohl Andre Laarson, the young Norwegian genius who had become extraordinarily wealthy by harnessing electromagnetic rays, replacing fossil fuels and abruptly halting Climate Change, was paying for the entire enterprise through his company. Laarson had considered building his own spaceport, but the time needed was more daunting than the expense. In the end, he opted to rent the NASA facility, as SpaceX and others had done before him.

That had been Hathaway's recommendation. Laarson could be stubborn, but at least he was willing to listen to alternative ideas.

"PAL Industries didn't need to reinvent the wheel," Hathaway said to the reporters. "The facilities were here and available. As you probably know, because of orbital mechanics, trips to Mars are possible only every two years. If we missed this opportunity, we would have to wait another two years. Mr. Laarson isn't that patient."

"Why Mars?" another reporter asked.

Sighing quietly, Hathaway realized his entire introduction with multiple slides and explanations had been ignored by the media.

They just wanted to hear from the astronauts and had been too busy with the free refreshments to listen to anything a mere colonel said. "It's the lone rocky planet both close enough to be accessible and also able to support life," Hathaway finally answered. "Next."

"Noelle Effman, *Miami Herald*," another reporter said into the microphone. "As I understand it, you intend to dig into Mars and create some kind of underground city. Is there any concern about destroying possible life forms below the surface?"

Finally, Hathaway thought, a decent question. "Humans will have limitations living on the Martian surface. The average temperature, as noted earlier," he emphasized, "is minus eighty-one degrees Fahrenheit. While it can get to a balmy seventy degrees in the southern region in the summer, severe dust storms limit where we can survive. The radiation is also intense. In light of these factors, we envision a subterranean city. We are concerned about possible biota under the surface, but we have equipment to identify microscopic life forms and will do our best to avoid damaging any possible ecosystem."

Tunneling was bound to cause damage, Hathaway thought to himself. *What does Effman think? The astronauts are going to slip between the rocks?* "Next."

"Wayne Traffolt, Reuters," a tall thin man said, standing up. "Mars was much closer in twenty twenty-two and is now moving away from Earth. Wouldn't this expedition have been better served waiting until Mars and Earth were just fifteen million miles apart?"

Hathaway hesitated for a second. Traffolt was a well-known science writer. He already knew the answer. *What are you fishing for?* Hathaway wanted to ask but didn't. "The next time Mars will be that close to the Earth is twenty thirty-five. No one wanted to wait that long. This was the soonest PAL Industries could get the Odin rocket ready and the crew properly trained," he said.

"Didn't that mean rushing to complete everything before Mars was too far away?" Traffolt followed up.

Aha, Hathaway thought. *He's trying to claim PAL cut corners.*

"We would never put the lives of our astronauts in danger unless all systems are go," Hathaway insisted. "Next."

"Bettina Hilliard, Warren News," a middle-aged woman said standing up and grabbing the mic as though it were a club. "The crew may be leaving from Cape Canaveral, but they will be flying the PAL Industries flag. Are we to understand Laarson intends to claim Mars and keep any resources for himself?"

Hathaway couldn't help himself and gave a muffled, scornful laugh. That canard had become internet fodder in recent days building up to this media event. He had no idea why anyone would concoct such a story or even try to denigrate this epochal launch. He also knew all about Hilliard, who seemed to delight in spreading false reports.

Speaking slowly and clearly as if addressing a child, Hathaway said, "As you know, Ms. Hilliard, the rocket will be flying under the flag of the United Nations, not PAL Industries. Mr. Laarson has no designs on Martian resources and is only fulfilling a boyhood dream of exploring Mars. He's realistic and knows he cannot go; sending these two brave people is the next best thing."

Hilliard wasn't done. She held onto the microphone with both hands. "We heard Laarson was really dead and his ashes will be left on Mars," she said. "That this whole thing is just an elaborate burial plan. Is that true?"

The runner seized the microphone before she could continue.

"Let me assure you, and anyone else who may be wondering; Mr. Laarson is very much alive. There will be no ashes or human remains on the rocket," Hathaway said.

"Then where is he?" Hilliard shouted. Other reporters chimed in with various supporting noises.

Behind Hathaway, a large screen darkened as the closed-circuit image of the speaker vanished and then brightened as Laarson's familiar face appeared. Reporters sat up, almost in awe. Gasps filled the room. The governor virtually saluted. One of the movie stars, shimmering in a golden dress, batted her eyes and arched her back in a sensual pose. In the front row, Hilliard just gaped. Her jaw moved up and down before clamping shut. One reporter, popping grapes in his mouth, continued to feed himself but did not swallow. He quickly resembled a chipmunk. The shrimp-devouring senator almost genuflected.

"Thank you for expressing concern about my wellbeing," Laarson said with his familiar accent. "I am not there now to avoid shifting attention away from the two courageous astronauts who deserve it more. However, as you can see, I have been watching the proceedings."

"How do we know that's not a tape?" Hilliard demanded. Hathaway marveled at how loud she was without a microphone. She placed both hands on her waist and glared at Hathaway then at the screen. No one said anything. Stunned faces shifted from Hilliard to Laarson and back.

Amid the silence, a somber, middle-aged man in a tuxedo walked down the center aisle. His shoes clicked loudly against the hard surface. Despite drawing everyone's attention, he maintained a steady, unhurried pace. In a moment, he reached Hilliard's side. She glanced at him. He held out a letter. She looked at it and at him. The man didn't speak. Hilliard finally took the envelope.

"Please open it," Laarson said. He was smiling.

Hilliard complied. She placed the envelope in her chair after extracting a piece of paper. The room waited. Even the reporter with a mouthful of grapes stopped feeding himself. One of the actresses took advantage of the moment to stand and smooth her dress. She snuck in a small wave in Laarson's direction before sitting down and ostentatiously crossing her legs. In the front row, Hilliard slumped into her seat and looked up at the screen in open-mouthed wonderment and then back at the letter.

"Ms. Hilliard, perhaps you are unaware that I now own Warren News," Laarson said. Hilliard glumly shook her head. "I do admire people who follow orders, however illogical and distasteful they may be," Laarson continued. "However, as the letter states, you are dismissed." Hilliard retained the same shocked expression. Her makeup cracked on her forehead, and her mascara started to run. "I am not a hard person," Laarson continued. "I do not like to make women cry. So, I will have a list of job openings sent to you. Meanwhile, we will continue with the media conference." He smiled. "The mission must go as planned. *Å få blod på tannen.*"

He faded away and was replaced by a view of the stage.

"What does that mean?" a reporter asked. Hathaway could see the puzzled faces. A couple of Norwegian representatives nodded, but no one else understood. "Mr. Laarson is saying he won't allow anything to interfere with the flight to Mars." That was as good of an interpretation of "blood on my tooth" as anything, Hathaway thought. He had learned a lot of Norwegian idioms. Working for Laarson, he had no choice.

Hilliard showed the letter to the reporter next to her, who

quickly passed on the information. Hathaway maintained his firm expression, despite misgivings. Laarson liked such grand gestures and obviously heard of the negative Twitter, Facebook and other social media commentaries. Still, Hathaway had no doubt upcoming news accounts would focus on the Warren reporter and less than he desired on the mission.

"Are there any more questions?" Hathaway asked. His voice radiated around the room and seemed to re-animate the crowd.

Hands went up. The discussion continued. Quietly, Hilliard stood up and left the room, leaving the empty envelope on her vacant chair. Hathaway watched her. *This has to be a setup*, he thought. After all, Laarson must have arranged for the letter to be delivered. Even he couldn't get that accomplished without advanced planning. What was he thinking? Hathaway didn't know. How like Laarson to fire her and simultaneously offer her a different job, Hathaway decided. Why did Laarson want Hilliard on the payroll? Hathaway could only envision problems ahead with that decision.

Hathaway turned back to the crowd. From the dais, he could see how excited Arti's parents still were. They only quivered as they leaned forward and stared at their son. Hathaway wished Kate's parents were as enthusiastic, but then, he thought, maybe they had the right idea staying away. The headaches were just starting. He was overseeing a massive operation to get two humans off the planet in a small, experimental rocket that would largely rely on concentrated electromagnetic rays for energy and to get them to Mars and, eventually, back home. That was a big enough challenge. For starters, would the rocket even function properly? It had in several tests, but PAL was relying on computer models. Hathaway almost shivered at the thought of everything that could go wrong. He and his team had tried to think of every contingency but knew that was impossible.

After all, he hadn't imagined Hilliard would get involved.

CHAPTER 3

Nearly two weeks later, Hathaway sat in the small, glassed room and studied the two astronauts on the other side of a clear glass panel. They were meeting less than four hours prior to liftoff. Neither seemed agitated. Both maintained their composure, sitting in military fashion with backs rigid. Kate and Arti were watching him, but, as Hathaway well understood, their minds were elsewhere. Maybe they were thinking about parents and siblings safely away from the launch site but with a clear view. Kate's parents had deigned to attend the launch along with their son. Laarson owned a very persuasive checkbook.

Arti's parents, on the other hand, left Cape Canaveral only once each day and that was to spend the night in a nearby motel. Two older brothers had flown in. They spent a lot of time badgering officials for increased benefits for their son, who could not have known about their efforts. They even called Laarson's office, but did not get through. Every time the parents showed up, staff generally scurried to avoid contact or to appear too busy for a conversation. Hathaway often needed to interfere and assure the parents their son was receiving every consideration. They were not easily deterred or satisfied.

Hathaway was pleased neither astronaut was married. He didn't want to imagine what kind of trouble spouses might have caused.

Both astronauts said their goodbyes to their relatives a week ago before heading into quarantine to reduce chances of catching any illness. Covid 19 and its variations may have been largely tamed via vaccinations, but it still remained a threat.

Both astronauts had passed their physicals before entering the bisected, decontaminated briefing room for final instructions. Hathaway smiled at Kate and Arti. They only acknowledged his presence with their eyes.

"I don't want you to worry about anything," Hathaway said. "You are trained; you know what to do."

"I would like to walk out first," Arti blurted. He did not look at his partner. Hathaway realized the Armenian must have been thinking about not losing face by following a woman. By rights, the commander should lead the crew to the ship. Did it matter?

Hathaway turned to Kate. "Is that all right with you?" he asked.

Kate nodded. A small concession, Hathaway decided. How many more would Arti request?

"Arti, I remind you Commander Khatun is the leader of this mission," Hathaway said. "Mission Control will relay directions to her."

"Yes, sir," Arti said, before shifting slightly to salute Kate.

"Arti," Hathaway said, "I also shouldn't have to tell you this mission can be aborted if there are disruptions."

"I won't be the cause, sir," Arti promised with apparent sincerity.

"Of course not," Hathaway replied. He was glad Arti didn't smirk. After all, the launch really couldn't be halted. Not only was timing tight to avoid a solar conjunction when the Sun stood between Earth and Mars, cutting off all communication for two weeks. At the same time, the distance between the two planets was growing wider. Soon, the journey would take too long to contemplate. In addition, PAL was paying about $30 million for the launch and had invested $100 million to develop the rocket, which was smaller and lighter without the millions of pounds of fuel. Millions more were being spent on training, development of the landing capsule, food and supplies. The astronauts were aware how much this trip cost. Hathaway continued to harp on the need to follow set protocol without deviation. However, he also knew his comments rang hollow. Once in space, far from Earth, the astronauts would have to improvise amid unforeseen circumstances.

Shifting topics, Hathaway carefully went over the launch sequence, reminding the astronauts of the controls and the escape procedures. They showed no fear. They had practiced shutting off the engines and steering to a landing in the closest body of water, although the idea such action may become a necessity had to be chilling. Hathaway watched their faces, but they remained stoic. Danger, after all, was built into these kinds of assignments. Every day, inside the training center atrium, they passed a memorial to fallen astronauts.

Because electromagnetic rays from space would provide most of the power, Hathaway reminded them the ship didn't have more than a small amount of the liquid oxygen/liquid hydrogen fuel needed to create initial thrust. Once liftoff commenced, the ever-present electromagnetic rays would propel the rocket. A fully loaded rocket weighed more than 6 million pounds, including 1.1 million pounds of fuel; the Odin weighed in at a little over 1 million pounds. The smaller, lighter ship had room for important equipment, including an oxygenator which would be used to split the carbon dioxide that dominated the Martian atmosphere into component parts, creating sufficient oxygen for the crew. Nitrogen would be siphoned from space and also carried in tanks to mix with the oxygen, bringing the mixture closer to Earth standards. There was also an exercise room so the two astronauts could maintain their health and stamina enroute as well as a game room with films and music.

Hathaway repeated what the astronauts knew: the Odin would also make the 39-million-mile trek in around 4 months, traveling at close to 14,000 mph. The Martian rovers needed seven months to make the journey, but they weighed less than 2,000 lbs. Odin may be bigger and heavier, but it would also travel at a faster rate of speed. As Hathaway pointed out, the speed was unusual for a manned flight, but not inordinate. To clear Earth's atmosphere, rockets needed to exceed 25,000 mph. The Shuttle topped 17,000 mph to remain in Earth orbit. The crew of Apollo 10 set a record on their journey back to Earth at more than 24,000 mph. Then, too, the Parker Solar Probe topped out at 430,000 mph. The probe only weighed 1,500 lbs. So, Hathaway stressed, Odin's speed would not be excessive. Even better, the probe withstood intense radiation, internal vibrations and coldness of space before getting blasted by the sun. That same technology had been transferred to Odin.

The Odin's outer shell, which was composed of Kevlar, aluminum, carbon-carbon composite, silica and thermal glass, had been tested and deemed capable of surviving the journey. Practice flights with robots had gone well; so had low-level tests with humans. Yet, as Hathaway well knew, Columbia in 2003 appeared to be functioning perfectly until foam broke off from the external tank, breached the Shuttle's wing and ended in the death of the seven astronauts aboard. Their names were on that atrium memorial plaque as a daily reminder to this crew.

As a result, Hathaway continually reminded himself that something seemingly insignificant could doom the ship, especially at the planned speeds and exposure to the hazards of space; none of which could be perfectly duplicated on Earth. PAL engineers could only hope the Nomex felt insulation inside the rocket's mostly aluminum shell would hold up as well on a long flight as it did in tests. After all, Voyager 1 had journeyed the full length of the solar system at 33,000 mph and survived. Voyager 2 had followed suit.

The astronauts had studied all of that. Their steady gazes assured Hathaway Odin's durability was not one of their concerns.

Hathaway then shifted to their health. Astronauts on shorter missions reported gastrointestinal problems when they landed. Doctors found changes in the brain. Some even aged prematurely. Neither Kate nor Arti seemed upset. NASA had come up with an exercise program and diet that was supposed to reduce the impact. The astronauts also had tremendous confidence in their own conditioning to handle any physiological effects. Undaunted, Hathaway reiterated the information.

He then turned to their journey from Odin to the Martian surface. Once in orbit around Mars, Kate would separate the capsule or MEM (Mars Excursion Module, nicknamed MOM by the astronauts) and descend to the ground. Parachutes would be deployed to slow the entry. Odin would remain in orbit under automatic pilot in conjunction with Mission Control. On the Martian surface, Kate and Arti would erect a small, inflatable building for protection and begin boring through the crust, taking samples to be tested later and beginning the process that would end with the colonization of the Red Planet. The alternative energy source meant the capsule had room enough to carry the necessary equipment and food.

Hathaway could see the astronauts' eyes glaze over but persisted in reminding them of the details. He could hardly claim to have done his job without emphasizing important aspects of the flight and landing.

"You will be monitored at all times," Hathaway said. "However, as you move away from Earth, the time delay between communication will go from three minutes to fourteen minutes. Remember that."

They both nodded. However, Hathaway noted, Arti rolled his eyes while Kate decided the wall was more interesting. Seeing their reactions, Hathaway dropped the remaining recap and asked about their families. Kate said nice things without any enthusiasm; Arti bubbled with appreciation for his parents' excitement and mentioned his two brothers were on hand for the launch.

After a few more minutes of idle conversation, Hathaway sent them to don their space suits. He went back to his office with three computer screens and access to the tremendous glut of statistics. Sitting behind his large desk, he put on his headphones and called Mission Control where Consuelo served as his constant contact. The other lines connected him to Laarson's headquarters in Norway and to his own secretary at the space center. He only had to push the correct button.

"All systems go," Consuelo reported.

Hathaway scanned the readouts flickering in front of him. Every instrument glowed green. NASA engineers were running the launch and would monitor the ship's equipment during the long trek through the solar system. Hathaway then looked at the digest of media accounts collected by his secretary. Every news outlet seemed focused on the launch.

Aware how smooth the operation was going, Hathaway almost relaxed but cut off that emotion before it overtook him. The launch, flight, landing and return was his responsibility. Unlike Atlas, Hathaway could not see a way to remove that weight from his shoulders. The strain was exhausting, augmented by his inability to sleep well. His wife had arranged for several massages, but they did little to ease the stress he was feeling.

He sat down in his stuffed leather chair and turned on its heating element. Soon, he felt the warmth begin to caress his lower back. Reaching across his desk to the closest computer, he shifted its camera to the staircase leading to the rocket and checked his watch.

Exactly 150 minutes before launch, Arti led Kate down the entryway into the module on the tip of the new Odin rocket. Hathaway watched them carefully with a mixture of pride and parental worry. Kate's smaller figure, clad in a white suit emblazoned with the blue and white United Nations' flag on the back, walked confidently. Arti, wearing an identical suit, marched in a more formal pose with his shoulders square and arms almost rigid by his side.

Finally, Hathaway thought, *it's happening.* All these years after Laarson first proposed the journey, the hard work and determination had finally led to this moment. However, Hathaway didn't feel any sense of relief. That would have to wait until the two astronauts returned. Instead, he had a sense of stepping into an abyss along with Kate and Arti.

Hathaway checked his watch again. Norway was six hours ahead—late afternoon there. Pressing the first button, Hathaway called Laarson in his Stavanger office and was immediately put through. Laarson appeared on the computer screen, smiling, as usual. Hathaway noted his boss was dressed in a white jumpsuit, mimicking the astronauts.

"*Hei*," Laarson greeted him with a broad smile. "How is media coverage?"

"Excellent," Hathaway replied. Media representatives from around the world had flocked to Florida. Hathaway had ordered thousands of media packets in preparation, but didn't know if there were enough given the intense interest. Camera crews were set up at every vantage point. Security reported spectators had filled the causeway, stopped traffic on 1-95 with the sheer volume and clogged every available space. Helicopters hired to survey the area reported viewers filling beaches up and down Florida's east coast. The Atlantic Ocean was covered with boats, and airport controllers were keeping busy directing small planes away from the launch site.

That morning, NASA veterans said they'd never seen so many people excited by a launch. "How often did you send a man to Mars?" Hathaway had asked them. That easily trumped the Moon launches, they agreed.

"From what I'm hearing, it looks *utmerket*—excellent," Laarson said. "In publicity alone, we've almost made up the cost."

"Do you need more publicity?" Hathaway replied without thinking and immediately regretting saying anything.

Laarson just laughed. "*Høhøhø*. That's why I like you, John. You cut to the heart of everything." He gave the sly grin Hathaway knew well. "By the way, I am getting you a publicity assistant," Laarson said. "You are very busy. I am sure you need someone to handle reporters."

Hathaway waited. Someone else to keep track of? He didn't say anything. The enormous salary PAL Industries paid him compensated for any misgivings he might have, especially when addressing reporters. They all seemed to be determined to expose his lack of a space-related background. "Who?" he asked.

"Bettina Hilliard," Laarson said. "She will be in the media center for the launch."

"I haven't briefed her," Hathaway protested, feeling a cold chill at the sound of Hilliard's name.

"I did," Laarson said. "You can do your job. She will do her job."

Hathaway shook his head and stared at the carpeting. "Yes, sir," he mumbled. The call ended.

For a moment, Hathaway didn't know what to think. Hilliard? In the newsroom? The woman was a pest from the first day he met her. Laarson may admire loyalty, but who was Hilliard loyal to? Hathaway shifted his attention back to the launch. He had no time for such distraction. How like Laarson to throw something at him at the last minute.

He could hear the voice of Launch Control over the loudspeaker: "T-minus one hundred twenty minutes and counting." Then came the dizzying checks of every aspect of the launch, repeating what had been done before and would be again. Representatives from every sector would have to agree the launch was clear to go before liftoff took place. Launch and Mission Control would see to that.

Feeling his tension rise, Hathaway continued to study the instruments. Laarson had found him after Desert Storm died down, and he eagerly took the PAL job, retiring from the Air Force as a Lt. Colonel with a full pension. His skill at organizing and maintaining schedules guaranteed, as PAL's the space program evolved, he would find himself in a key role. Soon, he was running it.

Even so, the various indicators remained something of a mystery, no matter how much he studied them. He could only look for the green light accompanying the ever-changing numbers to feel in any way assured.

"T-minus ninety minutes," the voice intoned.

He flicked on the connection to Kate. He could hear her breathing. "Everything all right, Kate?" he asked.

"Roger," Kate replied. Her voice came through solid and clear, without hesitation.

"Godspeed," Hathaway said.

"Salaam," Kate said.

Hathaway signed off and smiled. Kate still had her sense of

humor despite the tense situation. She was Christian, not Islamic like Arti, but still adopted the Arabic word perhaps as a sign of camaraderie with her colleague or just for the sound of it. Hathaway didn't know. Regardless, the familiar word made him feel better.

He briefly wished Arti well, using the Armenian he had learned: "May Allah be with you. *T'vogh Allahy dzez het lini.*"

The astronaut thanked him in English.

Time dragged. Hathaway kept watching the clock, but it never seemed to move. On the various screens, computer experts and flight staff hurried about, watching flickering computers, constantly checking with each other. Hathaway remained isolated in his office with his array of monitors. He did not want to interfere. NASA personnel knew what to do and certainly did not need him in the way. His job was done for the moment, but he felt increasing nervousness as time neared for the launch. PAL only had the one rocket. The window between launches was such the next one wouldn't have to be ready for about two years anyway. Still, he wished another one was available.

In the Air Force, he always kept a backup in reserve. Not having one now increased the sandpapering of his nerves, as though he were missing something important. That nagging thought followed him everywhere.

"T-minus sixty minutes."

"Colonel," Consuelo said in Hathaway's earpiece. "There's a woman in Launch Control who is causing some problems."

"What!" Hathaway exclaimed, sitting up.

"T-minus sixty minutes and holding," the loudspeaker intoned.

"She says Laarson gave her permission," Consuelo continued.

"I don't care if God did," Hathaway thundered. "Get her out of there."

"Security is here. She's refusing to go," Consuelo reported.

"T-minus sixty and holding."

Hathaway stared at his monitor. It didn't show anything except some of the staff turning and looking to their right. He shifted the camera. He could see several security guards surrounding someone.

"Who is that?" he demanded.

"Some reporter," Consuelo said.

"How did she get through security?" Hathaway was appalled. If a reporter could wander in, maybe anyone could.

"I don't know. She had some kind of pass," Consuelo said.

One of the guards turned enough for the camera to focus on the culprit. Hathaway's jaw dropped. Hilliard. He felt sick. "Tell that woman to report to me immediately," he said. He watched as a security officer took Hilliard's arm. She tried to anchor herself. "I'm her boss," Hathaway said. "Tell her she's got five minutes to get up here or lose her job. I'll have her thrown off the tower if necessary."

Hilliard glared at the camera as the message was relayed and allowed herself to be led away.

"T-minus sixty and counting," the loudspeaker continued.

Still seething, Hathaway tried to calm himself. Any moment that woman was going to walk through his office door. He didn't want to talk to her. He didn't want to see her. He had spent several months fuming at the TV whenever she appeared with some cockamamie story about the launch. She launched pet conspiracy theories like balloons, blowing up another when one vanished. Now, she was working on the inside. Only the Lord knew what trouble she could cause.

He heard a knock on the door. Wei peeked in. "Ms. Hilliard is here to see you," she reported.

"Tell her…" Hathaway started. Wei maintained a blank expression. "Never mind," he said. "Let her in."

Wei nodded.

Red-faced and clearly upset, Hilliard walked in. "Lt. Col. Hathaway," she greeted him stiffly. Hathaway swiveled in his chair. She glared at him. Instead of the somewhat plain-looking woman in a suit as she appeared on TV, she had let her hair down and reduced her makeup. She was wearing a clingy dress as well. Hathaway wondered who she was trying to impress. He didn't care what she looked like. If she was intending to make his wife jealous, Hathaway knew Hilliard had the wrong target in mind.

"I am here, as you ordered," she said.

Hathaway looked away. "What the devil were you thinking? You know we're in the middle of the launch countdown."

"T-minus fifty minutes and counting."

"I wanted to be sure it wasn't a simulation, like when we supposedly went to the Moon," Hilliard said.

Hathaway felt a cold shiver and leaned toward her with an angry stare. "We went to the Moon nine times," he said in cold, clipped tones. "If the U.S. faked it, why nine times? Besides, the technology to fake a Moon landing didn't exist in nineteen sixty-nine And, finally, you…you…can take any telescope and you can see the equipment left on the Moon. Focus well enough and you can see the damn poop bags." He turned back. "Get away from me."

"Yes, sir," Hilliard replied. "Or should I say 'roger.'"

"You can call me Colonel," Hathaway said.

"I thought 'roger' meant…"

"I know what it means," Hathaway interrupted.

"By the way, I work for Mr. Laarson," Hilliard added. "Mr. Laarson wants me in the media center for the post-launch briefing. I have a pass from PAL Industries." She held up a card.

Hathaway stared at her. "I will talk to Mr. Laarson. I doubt he wants the launch delayed," he snapped. "Besides, you were in Launch Control, not the media center. You do know the difference, don't you?"

"Yes, sir," Hilliard said. "I was just following Mr. Laarson's directives."

Hathaway tried to ignore her. She was probably lying anyway. There was no time to contact Laarson to verify anything she said. "Stay away from Launch Control," Hathaway ordered. "And don't wander onto the launching pad. I won't care, but Laarson may not want to lose you."

"Of course," Hilliard said with a wry smile. "Do you mind if I stay here for the launch?"

Hathaway groaned inwardly. He did not want her remotely close to him. On the other hand, if she remained, at least he could keep an eye on her.

"Suit yourself."

Hilliard looked around and found an empty chair by the desk. She turned the closest monitor to face her. She stared intently at the numbers. Hathaway saw her rest her hands on the keyboard. He sprang to her side. "Don't touch anything," he ordered, imagining she would find some way to sabotage the launch.

She looked up at him. "Of course not," she said without any obvious rancor.

"Good," Hathaway managed and went back to his seat. Hilliard dropped her hands to her lap.

"T-minus forty-five minutes and counting."

Sweating, his pulse picking up, Hathaway tried to ignore her as the time dwindled down. A nagging thought tugged at him. She was going to do something; he just knew it.

CHAPTER 4

Two months later, Hathaway slipped into his office, relieved by the quiet that enveloped him. He sat down behind his desk and turned on the monitor. Behind him, on computers placed along the shelving, the readouts from the Martian voyage continued to run, changing constantly as the seconds ticked away.

Any moment, he expected Hilliard to walk in, complaining about something. He was sure she was still surreptitiously working for Warren News, which, despite new ownership, continued to spout nonsense. Hathaway spent much of his time squashing rumors Warren news anchors repeated as gospel. The resulting attention had kept the Martian expedition in the news, as if having two astronauts halfway to the Red Planet wasn't enough.

Hathaway clicked on the record icon. The sound of "Havana Gila" played in the rocket for 30 seconds. He made the mistake of playing music until either Kate or Arti responded, forgetting the time interval involved. Both were sick of "Good Morning Sunshine" by the time Hathaway ended that recording. He could see Kate in her bunk. She blinked and gave a weak smile.

"Hi," Kate said in Hathaway's headphone. She sounded very chipper despite nearly two months into the Martian trip. The sound and video now needed five minutes to reach Cape Canaveral. Hathaway felt odd living in the past. By now, Kate was probably getting dressed.

"Sleep all right?" Hathaway asked.

"All quiet," Kate said five minutes later, "as usual." She yawned and stretched. Hathaway noted she hadn't got out of bed—like his wife, who spent several minutes each morning deciding whether to get up or luxuriate under the covers for a few more minutes. A shadow moved across the bed, and then Arti appeared.

"Hi," Arti said and waved.

"Have a good breakfast," Hathaway said.

"Yum," Kate eventually said, swinging over the side of her bunk. Hathaway tried not to laugh. The astronauts had plenty of food, all dried and packaged. Today's menu called for cold roast chicken, mashed potatoes, enriched wheat bread, quince sticks and coffee. It sounded good, but didn't look appetizing.

Hathaway clicked off the monitor and shifted over to the news digest his staff prepared. The first item stunned him. Warren News reported mission control officials had interrupted what appeared to be a romantic encounter between the astronauts. Hathaway almost choked. The account read by anchor Troy Commons even quoted Hathaway as saying he had expected something like that to happen. "When boys and girls work together, sometimes sparks fly," he quoted Hathaway as saying.

Outraged, Hathaway immediately buzzed Consuelo. "Get that woman up here immediately," he sputtered, knowing there was no need for further identification. Consuelo knew who Hathaway wanted to see. Hathaway refused to call Hilliard by name. He was also sure Hilliard was behind such fake news.

Kate reappeared on his monitor. "I noticed something odd," she said. The camera shifted to show a radar screen with a sweeping line across it. "There's this dot that keeps moving." She pointed to something.

The image was not clear enough for Hathaway to spot anything. He pressed one of his control buttons. Consuelo answered immediately. "Kate has seen something on her radar screen," Hathaway told him, even though Consuelo was privy to the same communication.

"Roger that," Consuelo said.

"See if someone in the control room has picked up anything," Hathaway ordered.

"Already done," Consuelo said. "Nothing yet."

"Keep looking."

Hathaway re-established his connection to the spaceship. "We'll let you know if anything turns up," Hathaway told Kate. Someone knocked on the door. He was too preoccupied to respond. Wei popped her head in. He waved and got a quick look at Hilliard entering. She sat in the closest chair. Hathaway remained focused on the screen. A dot? He couldn't see any evidence of one.

"It's moving very fast," Kate said.

"I don't see anything," Arti chimed in.

Hathaway could see Kate point to the screen and then move her finger across it as if tracing something.

Arti stepped back. "Maybe," he said.

"It's really quick," Kate said. "It's off the screen now."

"A meteor?" Hathaway suggested.

"No one here has detected anything," Consuelo reported in Hathaway's ear.

Hilliard inched closer. Hathaway pointed at the visitor's chair. She sat down again.

"Kate says it's gone now," Hathaway told Consuelo. "Have someone monitor that area closely." NASA kept careful track of meteors and comets. Still, one could have slipped through detection.

"It's back," Kate announced. "Now, I can count four, five, six dots, maybe more. They seem to be moving in formation."

"Aliens!" Hilliard cried, jumping from her chair and rushing to the desk to stare at the monitor. Hathaway glared at her. Laarson deflected any request to fire her. Instead, at Hathaway's insistence, she was limited to providing regular updates for reporters, keeping interest in the Mars landing alive as time passed.

"Will you just shut up," Hathaway snarled at Hilliard. "There's no evidence…"

"There must be fifteen or twenty now," Kate said in her steady voice, as if viewing a park scene. "They seem to have separated into units."

"Where is Arti?" Hathaway asked. Arti was no longer in sight.

"He left for morning exercise," Kate answered after the usual duration. "He does that religiously."

"Get him back," Hathaway ordered. "He needs to know what's going on."

"Roger," Kate replied after the long pause. She seemed calm and unperturbed by the dots.

For five minutes, Hathaway frustratingly watched Kate studying her computer screen. The delay was becoming intolerable. He was living in the past; Kate and Arti inhabited the future.

Hathaway again asked Consuelo to check with Mission Control. He sat back, feeling anxiety seep through him. The ship had no weapons. At worst, the panel of independent experts convened long before the launch assumed planetary microbes would be the biggest danger, and, if existing, none of them had evolved to infect humans. The idea of some kind of alien presence had not figured into anyone's predictions.

"Can Kate take evasive action?" Hilliard asked.

"To some degree," Hathaway replied, anxiously studying the screen. The ship could function on electromagnetic rays that filled space but would need to get back to the correct path to reach Mars safely. Even a tiny directional shift would greatly affect the planned landing. They had alternative sites, but Hathaway and his team of experts would prefer MOM landing on the flat plain identified by a Martian rover and named Utopia Planitia. The low-lying land would facilitate entry into the crust.

"Nothing reported," Consuelo said. "Mission Control says the radar there hasn't detected anything unusual."

Hathaway grimaced. They should be seeing what Kate was watching. Still, the time delay was making everything difficult. "Are the dots too far away for our equipment to pick up the signals?" he asked. He could feel Hilliard next to him. The woman was almost quivering in excitement.

"They shouldn't be," Consuelo replied immediately. "Of course, our computers are synched with on-board radar."

"Is there someone we can check with, anyone with some experience in this sort of thing?" Hathaway asked.

"Mission Control has an advisor," Consuelo said. "I'll get back to you."

Hathaway studied the screen. If they were aliens and not just some stray rocks, could they mask their presence? Did they have some kind of shield? Some way to deflect radar? Science fiction writers predicted such things. Some advanced civilization might have the necessary technology to camouflage movement.

"They're gone," Kate announced.

"I don't see anything," Arti said.

"Sorry to interrupt your exercise routine," Hathaway said.

Five minutes later, Arti smiled into the camera. "There's plenty of time. We still have another two months," he said with a wink and left.

"I'll keep watching," Kate said.

"We can monitor from here," Hathaway said. "Why don't you go work out or something?"

"After Arti finishes," Kate eventually said. "I don't like to bother him."

The screen abruptly went blank. Hathaway stared at it. Again?

He was furious and frustrated. What was going on? All video and audio had ceased for the third time since the launch. The blackouts so far had only lasted a brief time, but no one at NASA or any agency working with them could find a reason. It couldn't be the solar conjunction. That would not happen for another year in Martian time, about six months in Earth measurement. Maybe there was a short in the system, one engineer suggested. The electromagnetic rays powering the ship might be filtering through the engine unevenly, another proposed. After all, the entire process was brand new. Nothing like this had ever been tried before on such a grand scale. Just a glitch, Hathaway tried to reassure himself.

Still, the wait was agonizing. What if the power never went back on? The backup system also shut down. If the audio and video didn't return, the two astronauts would be flying through the blackness of space without any means of communicating. He pressed buttons on the computer. No response. He cut off the power and re-booted. Two minutes later, the screen was still dark.

Hathaway felt the need to grab something, to do anything. The first time this happened, the pause was for maybe 10 seconds. The second time, it lasted just under a minute. Now, the delay seemed interminable. If he smoked, the ashtray would have been loaded with butts instead of lozenges. He began to clench his fists. Then, he remembered Hilliard's presence. Hastily, he composed himself and sat down. He cleared his throat and popped in a lozenge. The menthol cooled him enough to look under control, regardless of the way his stomach felt.

"What shall I tell reporters?" Hilliard asked, seemingly unconcerned about the blackout.

"You..." Hathaway seethed, remembering why he wanted to see her. He walked around his desk and towered over her. He tried to keep his voice steady, but even looking at her infuriated him. "Did you hear the filth Troy Commons spewed this morning?" he asked coldly, already knowing her answer.

Hilliard shrugged. "I'm not part of that network anymore," she said. "Besides, I'm too busy to watch TV."

Hathaway stifled a more intense reaction. "You get Commons on the horn and tell him there never has been anything romantic going on during the mission. You tell him I didn't say a word..." Hathaway enunciated carefully.

"We're back," Consuelo said in Hathaway's ear, "Mission Control thinks the dots could be meteors."

Hathaway gave Hilliard one more glare but returned to his desk. The computer screen showed Kate standing by the microwave, waiting for her meal to heat up. She seemed calm, as though the lack of communication had not fazed her.

"You got that?" Hathaway snarled at Hilliard.

"Do you have Troy's number?" Hilliard said in a light voice. "I haven't talked to him in months."

Hathaway clenched his fist. "Just do what you are told," he said. "I am sure you can find the number."

"What number?" Consuelo asked.

"I'm talking to that woman," Hathaway said. "Meteors?"

"That's what NASA is reporting," Consuelo said.

Hathaway relaxed slightly. "That's better," he said, seeing the image remained on his computer screens. "We can live with meteors. Is that definite?"

"No," Consuelo replied. "Best guess. Kelly and Simpson reported that."

Hathaway nodded. They should know: Kelly was the ranking astronaut, now retired from flying; Simpson was NASA's assistant director.

"Keep at it until we get something definite," Hathaway said. "We can't keep losing contact."

"Roger."

"Meteors," Hathaway emphasized to Hilliard.

"Should I tell the reporters?" Hilliard asked. "How about the blackouts?"

"Tell them the truth," Hathaway directed. "NASA thinks the dots are meteors. The immense distances sometimes cut communication. Maybe a meteor flew through the electronic beam. Who knows?"

"Or aliens," Hilliard said with obvious glee.

"Do not say that!"

Hilliard shrugged and went back to her chair. Hathaway continued watching his screen.

Kate was still talking as if nothing had happened. Hathaway waited. There would be a 7-minute gap soon. "Does the screen go off in Mission Control?" she asked after reappearing. Hathaway said yes. Five minutes later, Kate bit her lip. "I'll check things here. I am sure you have engineers working on it there."

She glanced at her scope. "More dots," she reported.

"Aliens," Hilliard breathed. "Wait until the reporters hear about that."

Hathaway jumped up to face her. "I told you not to tell anyone anything," he ordered as formally as possible, almost shaking in anger and frustration. "We don't know what the dots are. I told you Mission Control thinks they may be meteors."

"Really?" Hilliard asked, seemingly innocently. "That's not likely."

"I'm not a genius. I don't know. Neither do you," Hathaway said. "I just don't need some crazy story in the headlines. We are sending astronauts to Mars. That should be more than enough." Even while saying that, he knew better. Hilliard was not going to listen to him, and there was nothing he could do about it. She gave a fake salute and started to get up.

"Don't leave," Hathaway barked. Hilliard remained seated and placed her hands in her lap like an obedient child. Hathaway didn't say anything. She was mocking him. She smiled pleasantly.

Hathaway quietly seethed. She was sabotaging everything. He was sure of that. He took several breaths to slow his heart rate. "By God," he said, "if I find out you are feeding lies to Warren News, I'll launch you to Mars without a rocket."

Hilliard stood. "After you clear it with Mr. Laarson first, of course, Colonel," she said and walked out.

Hathaway didn't bother watching her. He had to think about the rocket hurtling toward Mars. For more than two months, other than those annoying blackouts, everything had worked perfectly. Now this. What could he do? He wasn't going to abort the mission. That could be done, but not because of some dots on a screen. On the other hand, what if the astronauts needed help?

He heard a buzz. Consuelo. He popped onto the computer screen in front of Hathaway. "Dr. Ellie Dennis," Consuelo said, introducing a small woman with dark features. "She teaches at the University of Edinburgh, specializing in extraterrestrial life."

"Astrobiology," Dennis corrected in clipped tones tinged with a Scottish accent.

"Got it, Dr. Dennis," Consuelo said.

"Colonel," Dennis said, looking somewhat austere in a blue dress. "I have studied the screens and cannot detect anything the commander has reported. However, aliens could have developed a kind of shield that prevents sightings at a distance. That way, Kate would detect their presence but no one on Earth could. Such technology is theoretically possible."

"What can we do?" Hathaway asked. He continued to his attention shift between the monitor with the images from the spaceship and the one with Dennis.

"I have studied that," Dennis said. "If they are aliens, they may be just observing. There is no life on Mars possible beyond something microscopic. We've never detected any shelters there that might reflect an alien base. Perhaps they see Mars as part of their territory. Until we see any further activity, I would suggest we simply observe as well. They may be doing the same to us."

Hathaway considered that.

"Look at it this way," Dennis said, slipping into teaching mode. "Would this be any different than native Americans greeting Europeans? Both would have seemed inconceivable to the other. Or the Aztecs with the European explorer they named Quetzalcoatl. Cook in Australia with the Aborigines. Stanley in Africa with various tribes who had never seen a white man before. They must have watched each other warily at first."

Still, there were differences, Hathaway mused. The aliens—if that's what they were—had to be miles from Mars, too far for any direct contact. Columbus, Pizarro and the others had proximity in their favor. The aliens could also be more technologically advanced, something the Europeans didn't have to worry about. They could communicate with signs and gestures. Kate and Arti couldn't even flash colors, as was proposed in various movies.

"If I were an alien, observing a strange object, I would be very careful," Dennis said. "I would want to know what level of weaponry I would be facing."

"There isn't any," Hathaway said.

"They don't know that," Dennis said. "They may just circle and try to determine what kind of danger the ship represents."

"That's all speculation," Hathaway said.

Dennis looked peeved. "What do you expect? We haven't exactly got a long history of alien encounters of the first, second or third kind except in movies."

Of course, Hathaway thought, annoyed at himself. How could he allow himself to say anything so stupid? Dennis definitely wasn't impressed. "Apologies, I wasn't thinking," he told the professor.

"Many of my students forget *Star Trek* isn't a documentary," Dennis said.

Hathaway couldn't tell if she was being polite or sarcastic. However, her comments about aliens possibly seeing the ship as a threat chilled him. He felt extremely nervous. Unlike facing well-armed U.S. aircraft, the aliens might realize the Odin rocket could be blasted into smithereens without anyone being able to intervene. Maybe.

He thanked Dennis, immediately shifting the screen before she could respond by pressing the button to talk to Laarson. He didn't answer. Hathaway then jabbed the black button on his desk. Laarson's secretary, Heidi Nielson, appeared on his monitor.

"I need to speak to Pohl," Hathaway said.

"Yes, sir."

After a moment, Hathaway heard the familiar voice. "*God morgen*," Laarson said. He was sitting in a lab with an array of glass tubing in front of him. Hathaway filled him in about the dots. Laarson listened.

"I didn't think of that possibility," he mused. "That Kate is really creative."

"I'm sure she saw something, sir," Hathaway said.

"*Selvfølgelig*," Laarson said. "Of course."

"I want to order a speedup on the second rocket," Hathaway continued. "I need your permission for that."

"Another rocket?" Laarson mused.

"They may need help," Hathaway said. "We have to anticipate everything."

"Why did you not think of that before?" Laarson asked.

Hathaway almost erupted in anger. He had suggested getting a second rocket ready to go a full two years ago, but Laarson rejected it. Hathaway thought of an Air Force general who did the same thing to him: deny a plan and then criticize the fact nothing was done. Hathaway quickly gave the necessary documents to the Chief of Staff, who allowed the general to retire. Laarson faced no such consequences.

Hathaway realized quitting was an option, but that wouldn't solve anything. He needed to focus on the two humans now halfway to Mars and possibly in need of help. Frantically, he tried to think of a way to get Laarson's approval. He loved publicity. That might be sufficient.

"Can you imagine how the media will lap up a story about sending a rocket to save our brave astronauts?" Hathaway finally said. "That would trend worldwide."

"A rescue mission," Laarson mused. "I like that."

"I hope it doesn't come to that," Hathaway said. Actually, it couldn't. There was enough food to sustain the two astronauts for the four months needed to return home, but not to wait until the next ship arrived. The rescue mission wouldn't be ready for many more months anyway. He didn't tell Laarson that.

"Now you are thinking," Laarson said. "Go ahead with the rocket. I will send authorization directly to Boeing." He grinned. "By the way, I just bought Amazon. Too bad, they cannot deliver to Mars." He left the screen.

Hathaway grabbed his cell phone and called the Boeing plant in Huntsville, Alabama. The director of engineering Hal Worthington came to the line in minutes. The company needed another six months at least to complete the stages of the next rocket, he reported. Hathaway could see puzzlement in Worthington's eyes. He appeared concerned, obviously wondering if something had gone wrong with the rocket en route to Mars. He knew full well media reports did not contain inside information.

"We don't have that long," Hathaway said. "We have to go twenty-four/seven. I want that rocket launched in three months." Before Worthington could say anything, Hathaway continued. "Laarson's orders," he said. "Authorization is on its way."

"What's the rush?" Worthington asked.

Hathaway hesitated. He couldn't lie to Worthington; he knew far more about the spaceship than Hathaway did. On the other hand, the possibility of aliens couldn't be bandied about. He did know if Worthington could keep that quiet. "It doesn't matter," Hathaway said. "Don't cut corners, but get it done."

"Yes, sir," Worthington said.

Hathaway returned to the astronaut's monitor. Kate was staring at her computer.

"They're back," she said, gesturing toward her radar sweep. "And they are getting closer."

Then Hathaway's screen went black again.

CHAPTER 5

Alone in his office, his eyes focused on his desk monitor, Hathaway intently watched the image of the module separating from the huge rocket. The two astronauts would descend to the Martian surface while their ship continued in orbit above them. He could see MOM moving away. Although seemingly tiny alongside Odin, the module contained a storage area as well as food supplies.

Kate seemed very confident. As planned, ignoring any possible alien interference, the astronauts were landing on the Jezero Crater, located in the northeast quadrant of the planet. It wasn't the planned site but seemed a better option. The rover Perseverance had mapped the area, which was thought to be a dry riverbed. However, the location created a 14-minute delay for the video and audio to arrive on Earth.

Anything could happen in that time gap, Hathaway realized. On Earth, they had talked about the time delay for months before the launch. Then, it had just seemed like an abstract obstacle easily overcome. Now, the reality added to the tension. He sucked hard on a lozenge and tried to maintain a calm demeanor. Everything was going smoothly, despite three more stomach-churning episodes of communication blackouts. No one could figure out why; but the engineers were sure the cause lay within the ship. They hoped the capsule's equipment would not have the same problem. So far, Hathaway noted, the blackouts had not followed the two astronauts into the capsule.

The dots had stayed away, too. Dennis was chafing to tell the public, eager to become a media darling. So far, however, the news of possible alien contact had not leaked out. Hathaway banned Dennis from all talk shows and the media. She reluctantly obeyed. Hathaway trusted her. With every passing day, however, Hathaway feared the worst. Hilliard was still repeating the meteor account, but also receiving the latest updates. She was worse than a sieve. Being threatened with being tied to the nosecone of the next rocket seemed to have muffled her for the moment.

Hathaway focused on the large computer screen on his desk.

After the module landed, it would soak up enough electromagnetic rays to be fully charged for the return to the ship. The astronauts had 6-days' worth of food aboard, the inflatable building, a device to mix soil and water into a slurry to cover the building's walls and the necessary equipment to drill into the Martian crust along with the oxygenator and the nitrogen containers. With a few hours' effort, they should be able to create a large enough cave, the first step to hollowing out Mars and creating an underground city, intended to lie about 10 kilometers below the surface.

Those distant dots, however, could undercut all their plans.

Relieved by the capsule's successful entry into the weak Martian atmosphere, Hathaway continued to study Odin's radar readings for any sign of the dots, whatever they were. Consuelo was monitoring the screens inside Mission Control. While Hathaway wanted to hear something through his earpiece, he also dreaded receiving a report of an attack.

So far, nothing. Whatever the dots were, they had not approached the ship or interfered with the landing. Kate and Arti kept a close watch. Arti kept complaining the images were not readily visible, which Hathaway decided must be due to the astronaut's lack of familiarity with radar. Or, maybe, he was having problems with vision similar to that reported by other astronauts on shorter trips. Kate could have the same limitations. So far, however, she seemed unaffected. Her eyes tested at the top level. If she saw something, Hathaway decided, it was there.

After landing, the astronauts were forced to wait inside MOM. Instruments on board monitored radiation levels, as well as registering cosmic rays and solar winds. Fortunately, there had been no recent strong solar flares with their potentially lethal blasts and levels remained in the green area. However, radiation levels had already topped 22 millirads, way over what astronauts on the Space Station faced. Then, a proton event briefly jumped the needle to 100 millirads.

Hathaway immediately contacted Mission Control. "Kate is keeping a watch on the levels," Consuelo said. "They're safe. MOM can withstand the radiation. Their suits can handle twenty-two, but not one hundred. Kate knows that."

Somewhat reassured, Hathaway continued to watch the dials. He could see the radiation level dropping. The ship carried an inflatable building, and the astronauts were trained to use the Martian soil to create ceramic walls as barriers against the radiation. They would install the building, filling it with air from the oxygenator, and then start to dig a shaft underneath the building with the borer.

There would be no entry, descent or landing, however, until radiation levels fell to safe levels.

Hathaway grabbed another lozenge and stared at the instruments displayed on the monitors in his office.

"All systems go for EDL," Consuelo told him.

Hathaway couldn't relax. Kate had a 14-minute head start. By now, she may have already initiated descent to the surface. The module would need about 7 minutes to complete entry and landing. Back on Earth, they wouldn't know about it until the necessary time had passed. Hathaway glanced at the wall clock; half convinced the sweep hand wasn't moving.

"MOM has landed," Kate finally reported. Hathaway was thrilled to hear her voice and the triumphant sound radiating through it. She couldn't disguise her feelings, nor could he. A flood of emotions raced through him. Humans had arrived on a distant planet. This wasn't the Moon, a mere 239,000 miles away. No, two people had steered a spaceship close to 40 million miles and landed it on the rocky, red soil of another world in a little over four months. Hathaway felt a great swelling of pride.

The dedicated staff in Mission Control, in fact everyone involved with the mission, were no doubt cheering. Hathaway couldn't decide if he should join those here at the Cape; there was something special about relishing this moment alone in his office. He could see the monitor and knew Kate and Arti were getting ready to step outside. His screen showed them still in their seats as the module sat on Mars, but that was time delayed. By now, they were probably running various tests to determine if the soil could support them. Arti would be collecting the borer as well as the inflatable building. Mentally, Hathaway went through their checklist.

"No small steps anymore," Kate said in his ear, 14 minutes after saying those words on Mars. "This is a giant leap for women and men." Hathaway almost laughed aloud. She wanted to play off Neil Armstrong's famous—and often misstated—announcement when he first stepped on the Moon. Hathaway did not dictate anything and left the wording to Kate. Now, he forwarded the recorded words to the media center.

"The ground is firm," Kate reported. "MOM is sitting on volcanic basalt. Red dust flew up when we landed, but did not affect MOM."

Finally, Hathaway could see them on the screen. Both astronauts were standing on the ground in the image taken by the camera in the cockpit. Hathaway could only see their backs. He watched them go back to the capsule and release the cords to the parachute that slowed their entry. Their shadows were visible as they opened the storage unit in the back of the capsule.

Breathing hard, Kate was directing the process. Gravity on Mars was little more than a third of the Earth's, but the equipment was still bulky and heavy. Kate had nicknamed the borer "Worm," an idea drawn from the science fiction book *Dune*, but that didn't reflect its actual weight. Also, despite their rigorous exercise program, both astronauts still needed time to adjust to gravity and walking. Nevertheless, they managed. Kate almost fell once, but Arti caught her.

Hathaway watched them carefully. They were struggling with the equipment but did not seem fazed. Both were panting. Astronauts returning from time spent in the Shuttle, on the Space Station or Moon had lost weight and muscle mass. The Martian crew would likely have similar problems, Hathaway concluded.

"Building is inflating," Kate announced.

Hathaway stared at the monitor. The oxygenator must have worked. Laarson's electromagnetic engine seemed to be functioning properly even on a distant planet. Hathaway wanted to feel a sense of relief, but the possible missteps that had been considered on Earth remained in play. A sandstorm could sweep away the building before it was anchored. Engines could become clogged. The hard polymer fabric of the building might tear. The astronauts could have difficulty anchoring it in place. At least, it would help shield against excess radiation.

Inpatient, Hathaway waited, watching the building slowly inflating while aware anything could have happened in the 14 minutes since the video was sent.

Then, the building was standing. Hathaway could see it clearly in Kate's helmet cam. The structure seemed unsteady but was held in place with ropes and spokes fitted into grooves on all sides. Next, the 3-D printer rolled to the site would combine the soil and magnesium oxide with water plucked from the air to produce a ceramic-like covering. Once the shed was in place, the astronauts could put supplies inside and begin boring into the Martian surface.

The process of cloaking the building took several hours. The astronauts rested after that. Hathaway didn't send any directions. They seemed to be handling everything. The big thing, as far as he was concerned, was the machinery running on electromagnetic rays was functioning without any apparent problems.

Kate described the feeling of resting on Martian soil while hearing the wind pummeling the sides of the building. "It's almost like sitting on the beach, but facing away from the water," she said. "By the way, I did a bio check, nothing showed up."

Hathaway noted that. No life forms were being hurt. He sent a note to Hilliard in the media center.

The building filled with oxygen and Arti unsealed the nitrogen container. The astronauts were able to remove their helmets after their meters registered sufficient oxygen to breathe. Hathaway had cautioned them to try only briefly and one at a time. If something went wrong, they may not have enough time to put their helmets back on.

Still, seeing them sitting inside a building, with Ari's helmet by his side, was astonishing. Hathaway made sure the image taken by Kate's helmet camera was sent to the media center.

Then, they were standing, holding the end of the Worm, which extended through an air flap in the side of the building. A separate tube would funnel the debris outside.

"We got it," Kate said. "Arti, swing that end around. Tilt it." Hathaway listened to her struggling. She was strong and handled the equipment in practice. Still, reality was always different, especially in a cumbersome suit while coping with the effects of space travel. "All set," she said. "Activate."

In a few minutes, Hathaway heard what sounded like a large engine start up. On the screen, he could see Arti holding the borer. He was having trouble maintaining control as the Worm shook. Kate was trying to help, but really couldn't control the machinery. Meanwhile, rocks and dirt began flying in all directions, but most exited via the tube.

"It's working," Kate exulted. She was still panting. "Worm has already cut through at least four or five meters. Over here, Arti," she directed. "We've got to make it wider on this side."

Hathaway didn't say anything. By the time he could offer advice, another 14 minutes would have passed, making anything he recommended would be outdated. Besides, the astronauts seemed to be handling everything smoothly. He almost relaxed.

Then the screen went blank. Hathaway fell back in his chair. He frantically pressed computer keys to no effect. "We're trying to re-establish communication," Consuelo said in his ear. "Mars will not revolve away from Earth for another two hours." Hathaway knew when that happened, all communication would be blocked. The same thing would happen if the astronauts were on the dark side of the Moon.

"Did anyone see anything in the instruments?" Hathaway asked. The computer on the module had been relaying information until the shutdown.

"No, sir."

"Something has to be causing this," Hathaway muttered. He did not mention the possibility of alien interference. Neither did Consuelo. If aliens could block the transmission, who knew what else they could do? Hathaway didn't want to think about it. Kate and Arti wouldn't have any way of knowing until it might be too late.

The video resumed after a five-minute pause. His pulse racing, Hathaway tried to breathe slowly. If these blackouts continued, he was going to have a heart attack.

Kate returned to the ship and emerged with a rope ladder. "We've got to hollow out the sides," she told Arti. "Point the Worm that way. Good."

Hathaway watched the borer slowly digging out an area beneath the surface and into the iron, magnesium, aluminum, calcium, and potassium that comprised the rocky crust of Mars. Arti was able to descend about three meters and then shifted Worm sideways. Kate anchored the rope ladder and joined him. She moved her head to let her helmet camera get a panoramic view, revealing a dark cavern a few meters wide in each direction. Arti continued to aim Worm at the sides, quickly increasing the open space underground.

"Tell Mr. Laarson the rays permeate the ground," Kate reported. "The Worm is fully powered. We should have a good-sized room in just a couple of hours."

Hathaway watched with delight. The two of them were doing exactly as they practiced. In no time, apparently, they would be able to create an area large enough to be used as a future base. This was going better than expected. Hathaway couldn't contain his enthusiasm and walked around his office in a burst of energy.

Success. He could hardly believe it. So much planning. So much work. He might even take a day or two off. The astronauts were only to test the surface and dig a short distance into the crust. After that, they would take some samples and head for home, while MOM's computers recorded everything, tested the atmosphere and collected information on the soil. Everything was working perfectly, Hathaway thought. He had never felt better.

CHAPTER 6

After an hour more of work, exhausting from the combination of bulky suits and the heavy Worm, the two astronauts rested. They went into the module and ate a meal. They toasted their success with wine from a box, which had been included in the meals just for this occasion. Kate did not drink very much, but Hathaway thought she'd enjoy something more enticing than water and powdered orange juice. Since Arti's religion forbade alcohol, Hathaway also included a nonalcoholic version. Arti stayed true to his faith. Kate said she didn't mind finishing off the wine. There wasn't much in the box anyway, she added.

Back in his office, Hathaway sipped an actual glass of wine. He felt wonderful. All those years of equipping Air Force bases scattered across the globe and being sure their crews had ample food and supplies had led to this. The checklists, the careful counting, the endless details. All he had to do was get these two astronauts home after they finished with the room, which would serve as a base for the next shipload of workers. Then, Hathaway knew, PAL would launch a series of ships and get enough manpower on Mars to build the first elements of a community. In Laarson's schedule, the next ship would bring miners and men used to working below ground. More ships would carry massive oxygenators to fill the interior with air, possibly under an airtight canopy. Engineers felt they could construct one large and strong enough to endure the Martian wind, space radiation and incoming meteorites. It would siphon oxygen from clouds in space, speeding up the colonization process.

In addition, Laarson envisioned an elevator shaft maybe three kilometers long to carry people from the surface to the floor of the new community, which he wanted to christen Tyr, after the Norse god of war. Hathaway suggested Freyr, the Norse god of peace. The final decision hadn't been made yet.

Hathaway called Laarson, who was watching his monitor although it was 3 a.m. in Norway. "*Ja,*" Laarson said immediately. "You deserve a bonus."

Before Hathaway could thank him, Kate said something in his ear. "The dots are back," she reported.

Hathaway quickly said goodbye to Laarson and checked his screen. He couldn't see any dots.

"What quadrant?" he asked, knowing Kate wouldn't hear the question for another 14 minutes.

"I see four breaking off," Kate continued. "They are getting closer." She sounded unruffled.

"Miguel?" Hathaway called Consuelo through the headphone. "Get me some kind of techie. If Kate can see something, we have to be able to detect it."

"Hello, Colonel," Hathaway heard a familiar voice. He grimaced. Dennis. That woman was everywhere. Hilliard could learn something from her.

"Can't we focus a telescope or something on Mars?" he asked her. "Hell, we spent nine billion dollars on Webb. It's orbiting the Sun, right? It's a lot closer to Mars than anything else. Shouldn't it show us something?"

"Certainly," Dennis replied. "Webb is aimed that way now. It's just not designed to look for alien spacecraft."

"What good is it?" Hathaway snapped.

"Webb can see the whole planet once every two years," Dennis said. "Besides, it's looking for ancient galaxies. The best it can do is identify chemicals in the Martian atmosphere. It's supposed to pinpoint extremely faint and distant targets, but Mars is bright and close."

"That's not much help," Hathaway said sourly. "What about Hubble?"

"Hubble can only capture larger images, at least twenty kilometers across. Small dots would definitely escape it. You're thinking of sci-fi movies with giant spaceships," Dennis said. "In reality, spaceships are limited in size because of fuel requirements."

Hathaway thought she sounded sarcastic. "I'm not a fan of sci-fi movies," he said through gritted teeth. "I just think technology should be able to help here."

"There's not much we can do," Dennis said. "The other telescopes in space are more specialized. Those on Earth are too far away."

"I thought the telescopes were supposed to look for alien life,"

Hathaway said.

"They are," Dennis answered, obviously proud of the effort.

"Well, we seem to have found it, Dr. Dennis, without a single telescope providing a bit of help," Hathaway told her.

"Maybe something will show up," Dennis said lamely.

Hathaway abruptly cut her off. He turned back to his computer where the module camera focused on the astronauts and shifted to the cameras on the orbiting ship.

Something flashed by the screen. He couldn't tell what it was.

Kate was still describing what was happening 14 minutes previously. "Four dots on the left, around eleven o'clock. Another five, no six, at two o'clock," she said. "I have visual sighting." She was breathing harder.

"Arti wants to get into the cave," she said.

Hathaway waited for Arti to say something. He could hear him breathing, but not talking. "He thinks we'll be safer underground," Kate said. "Arti, stay here. He wants to take some of the food to the cave. No. That's an order."

Stay or go? Hathaway couldn't decide what to advise. If they stayed in the capsule, they could quickly relaunch, join the orbiting ship and leave. On the other hand, until then, they were exposed and very visible. In the cave, they would be hidden. However, if the MEM was damaged, they would be stuck there with limited supplies.

"The building is just as visible as MOM," Kate was saying. Hathaway was struck by how calm she remained despite the situation. He might have panicked. It sounded like Arti was getting desperate. Hathaway was proud of Kate.

He wanted to say something to encourage her. What if this was an airbase under attack? What would he recommend? Get as many aircraft in the air as possible while ground crews defend against the attackers. Find a safe harbor. Where? MOM was exposed; so was the building. Maybe Arti was right; they could hide in the cave. They had to get there. That meant crossing maybe 50 meters of ground. Could they do it safely? What kind of weapons did the aliens have?

"Arti, put that away," Kate ordered. "What good is a flashlight? I know the beam might appear to be dangerous, but it's not. It could provoke a real attack." Pause. "Don't go outside. At least MOM has a metal hull. Our little building will collapse with a single hit."

Hathaway sat down; his energy dissipated. He stared at the

screen. He could see the images of the yellow-brown sky seen through MOM's camera. The long tubing from the Worm lay silently to the left of the MEM. The astronauts were still inside the module. When they looked at each other, Hathaway pictured scared faces behind the gold-tinted visors. Arti looked frozen.

Hilliard came through the door behind Hathaway. "Reporters know," she said.

Hathaway whirled. "Know what?" he asked.

"About the aliens," Hilliard said.

"How?"

"Someone figured out a way to tap into the audio feed," Hilliard explained. She came over to look at the screen. "What should I tell them?"

Hathaway slumped in his chair. He knew better. "What did you tell them?" he asked.

"Only what you ordered," Hilliard said. "The truth." Hathaway put his head in his hands. "You are due to answer questions in the media center in thirty minutes, Colonel."

"I'm busy," Hathaway said.

"Then they'll know something is up," Hilliard said.

Hathaway glared at her. He also realized she was probably right. Foisting off such an important topic on an underling would definitely cause journalistic senses to start firing. Still, the mere thought of talking to the media twisted his stomach. Large presentations were easier if unpleasant; intimate gatherings were not remotely enjoyable.

"I thought you were handling the media," Hathaway said wearily.

"The reporters want you," Hilliard said with a smug smile. "For some reason, they don't trust me." She strolled out.

Hathaway heard the door close. She seemed so unconcerned. She had to know what was happening. On the other hand, she couldn't do anything either. Neither could he. If something had happened to the astronauts who went to the Moon, at least help was just a few days away. On Mars, no one could get there in less than four months—and that was at best. The new rocket wasn't ready regardless.

Feeling ill, Hathaway grabbed another lozenge. He sat down and stared at the wall, the one holding his framed commission as well as the photo of his wife, himself and their son, Preston. The interlude didn't change reality. He knew there really was no choice. He had to face the reporters while Mission Control kept him updated. He went back to his monitor. Nothing new. Kate was still describing dots and hearing sounds. She was also cautioning Arti. They discussed options. Torn between keeping tabs on what was happening on Mars and his duties on Earth, Hathaway thought his insides were going to collapse.

He told Consuelo about the meeting with reporters. "Interrupt with any updates," he insisted. "Keep me informed."

Feeling grubby, Hathaway went into the bathroom and looked in the mirror. His face was drawn and thin, his eyes; bloodshot. Not enough sleep; too many worries. Aliens will do that to a person, he decided. That and Hilliard. He must have aged 10 years in just a few months.

Sweat had permeated his shirt. He tossed it aside, took a quick shower and then pulled a clean white shirt from the closet. The front pocket was embossed with an eagle insignia.

"Colonel," Consuelo said in his ear, "Kate reports seeing flashes of light. They could be shots."

Hathaway ran into his office and checked the monitor. Kate looked as bad as he felt. Arti was somewhere else. His camera only showed the side of MOM's wall.

"Tell them to remain in the module," Hathaway finally said. "There isn't a damn thing we can do from here."

He felt helpless. All of those years of shipping supplies and organizing logistics had led to this dead end. Two people who most needed his help were isolated and beyond reach.

He called Laarson, who interrupted a massage to talk to him. Hathaway explained about the media conference. He hoped Laarson would tell him to cancel it but knew well how the Norwegian loved publicity.

"I really don't want to talk about aliens," Hathaway admitted.

"*Tull*," Laarson said.

He knew the Norwegian word. Laarson used it a lot to dismiss criticism. "They may not be aliens," Hathaway tried.

"We can always correct it later," Laarson said. "Keep me informed."

"Yes, sir," Hathaway said wearily as the communication ended. That would be easy. Laarson kept tabs on everyone. Hathaway wouldn't be surprised if Hilliard wasn't a spy for just that purpose.

Glumly, he stepped into the corridor. Wei looked up from her desk and gave him a wan smile. "Have Dr. Dennis join me in the media center," Hathaway directed. Wei nodded and picked up the phone.

Hathaway didn't wait. He threw back his shoulders and straightened his back. Head erect, he marched into the media center, a low, square building with many windows.

When he walked in, heads swiveled. Conversations waned. Hathaway could feel the intense stares. Reporters scrambled behind the rows of computers and outlets. Hathaway could see a couple television reporters talking into microphones in front of men holding cameras on their shoulders. There weren't as many reporters as at the news conference or even a couple of weeks ago. Coverage had died down as the ship hurtled through space but never disappeared completely, not with Warren News constantly reporting fake, often titillating, information. The successful landing drew wide interest, of course. Then a good percentage of the media returned to more public interest stories, like which pseudo-celebrity was marrying, having a baby, divorcing or causing a ruckus to maintain attention. As a result, Hathaway quickly counted barely 15 men and women amid the five rows of desks.

He stepped onto the small riser and stood behind the podium. Several reporters rushed up to attach microphones. He waited and didn't introduce himself. They all recognized him.

The big screen on the back wall behind Hathaway was looping through a retelling of the launch.

Deliberately quiet, Hathaway ostensibly adjusted the microphone. He tested the sound by tapping the mic. It was working well. He saw Hilliard point to him and give a thumbs-up. Hathaway cleared his throat. The raspy sound rolled through the center amid complete silence.

He could feel all the eyes boring into him. He learned forward and slowly spoke, saying something he never could have imagined just a few weeks earlier. "I am here to report that, apparently, the astronauts may have had an encounter with aliens," Hathaway said as calmly as possible.

He could see the reaction, which ranged from shock to almost glee. Behind the reporters, he spotted Dennis walking in. He didn't acknowledge her. Instead, as she walked to the front, Hathaway explained the timeline from when Kate first reported the dots to the current situation.

"Are you sure?" a woman reporter asked through the microphone held by Hilliard.

"Yes," Hathaway said. "Commander Khatun reported seeing objects she called dots. We cannot determine what they are from our position on Earth. Mission Control suggested they were meteors. However, that explanation appears to be wrong since the commander also said the dots were coming closer to the MEM. They are showing organization and coordinated movements." Hathaway paused, expecting the reporters to pick up on the obvious implication. Instead, all he saw were blank expressions. Veteran aerospace reporters were probably at Mission Control. The rest lounged here where food and drink was plentiful. "Under the circumstances," Hathaway finally said, "we suspect they are intelligent life."

"Are the astronauts in danger?" a reporter shouted before Hilliard could bring a microphone to her.

"We do not know," Hathaway said. "We are monitoring the situation."

"What could they do to defend themselves?" another reporter asked. Hilliard sat down; the thicket of reporters defeated her efforts to bring the microphone into use.

"The MEM has shields," Hathaway said, not explaining the protection worked against radiation and wind, not armaments. "At the moment, they are inside there."

"What do we know about the aliens?"

Hathaway shook his head. "Very little," he admitted. "However, Dr. Ellie Dennis, one of the top experts in astrobiology, is here to answer your questions." He invited her onto the riser.

She stepped up. "Thanks for the heads-up," she whispered sarcastically. He tried to look innocent. She was annoyed he broke the news, but there was nothing he could do about it now.

She promptly launched into a long explanation about the possibility of extraterrestrial life and the necessary conditions for such life to exist.

"Has life been found on Mars?" a reporter finally interrupted.

Dennis looked at Hathaway. He moved behind the podium. "Commander Khatun activated instruments after landing and reported no evidence of biological lifeforms," he said.

Reporters nodded.

Dennis quickly returned to the microphone. "Of course, our equipment cannot detect all possible forms of biological life," she said. "Further tests will have to be conducted."

"The dots caught on radar seem unrelated to any potential life on the planet," a reporter noted.

Hathaway nodded and started to reply. Dennis immediately elbowed him aside. "Perhaps the dots represent aliens who are interested in the biota of Mars," she said "We will continue to monitor the situation. I will give regular briefings."

Good, Hathaway thought. He had better things to do. Dennis may think she's getting the upper hand, but he welcomed her willingness to deal with the media. Besides, she could see the monitors like anyone else allowed in Mission Control but had no access to the direct communication from Mars.

"Definitely shooting," Consuelo said in Hathaway's ear. "Arti is heading back to the building. Kate doesn't want him to go. Apparently, he took the flashlight and is aiming it at the UFOs. She told him weapons would have little effect on aliens shooting at them from space. He won't listen."

Hathaway walked to the side of the stage. "Did any shots hit the rocket?" he whispered, letting Dennis' voice further muffle his words.

"Negative. The onboard computer's readings have remained steady," Consuelo said. "The aliens seem focused on Kate and Arti. Oh." He paused. "Kate said MOM has been hit."

Hathaway felt his stomach sink. The astronauts could be stranded on Mars with little food. His head reeled. He glanced at the reporters. He couldn't tell them, not yet.

"Arti, stay here," Kate said in Hathaway's ear. "I can't do anything if you get hurt."

"Arti is outside," Consuelo said. His usual laconic voice now dripped with emotion. "Kate is, too."

"Oh, god," Hathaway moaned. He heard silence and suddenly realized everyone was watching him. Dennis had turned and glared, hands on hips. She looked exasperated.

Hathaway started to smile as if nothing was wrong. He waved at Dennis to continue. She faced the reporters.

"Arti is hit," Consuelo said. "Kate said he almost reached the building. She can't tell if he's still alive. He's lying face down. She's rushing back inside. We are getting data from his suit. His pulse is weak." He hesitated before continuing. "The readout shows the MEM is stable. All systems are functioning. There's still nothing on the radar."

Hathaway shivered. Either the aliens could mask their presence or were too far away to be detected. They must have incredible weapons to achieve pinpoint accuracy at such a distance.

He could not stand anymore. He sat down on the edge of the riser and stared at the side wall. The screen there depicted the astronauts smiling and waving during training and then getting their suits on. The last image showed them walking solemnly toward the ship, Arti in front. Then the video began the loop again.

The news would be out soon enough, Hathaway thought. Whoever accessed the audio before would know what was happening. Laarson had to be informed. He shifted to PAL and told Laarson he was talking to reporters now. His voice seemed so loud, echoing around the room.

"This is very exciting," Laarson said.

Images and ideas raced through Hathaway's mind. He could see Arti's face, so sincere, on the film playing behind him. Hathaway shifted to Hilliard's line and told her quietly to stop the film. In a moment, the screen behind the stage darkened. That matched his feelings.

"Is Arti all right?" Laarson asked. "What do the monitors say?"

"Nothing yet," Hathaway said, after glancing at the large screen on the wall next to him. "Remember, there's a fourteen-minute delay." He looked at the screen. It went blank.

"Forget that bonus," Laarson said. His line went dead, too.

"I don't like this," Consuelo said. "Mission Control is going crazy trying to restore contact."

The monitor lit up again. Art's helmet cam remained dark. His computer seemed to have shut off. Consuelo didn't provide an update; he didn't have to. Hathaway knew what the silent computer meant.

"Kate can't get MOM to activate because of the angle," Consuelo said. "She's going into the storage area, away from the forward window."

Now what? Hathaway tried to focus. Arti was dead. That seemed obvious. There was no way to bring the body back. Would Kate be next? No rescue ship could arrive for months. Besides, the rocket under construction wasn't armed. To do that would require a major design change, delaying a second ship even more. Would PAL even send a second ship, given the danger? Was Martian exploration over?

Hathaway finally stood uneasily. He walked quietly to the side; acutely aware everyone was watching him. He contacted his secretary and asked her to connect him to Arti's parents. The reporters could wait. The father answered. Hathaway asked the family to meet him in his office. They could be there in 10 minutes. Hathaway promised to join them.

"Is something wrong?" the father asked.

"Yes," Hathaway replied. His voice seemed eerily loud in the silent room, even though he almost whispered.

He heard only silence before the father spoke, "Verily we belong to Allah, and truly to Him shall we return."

"Amen," Hathaway said.

He did not contact Kate's parents. Not until there was some final word, he told himself. Besides, he didn't want to hear recriminations about sending a woman into space and other brusque comments her father had shared with reporters.

He walked back to the microphone, trying not to appear concerned. Dennis was staring at him. Hilliard was not moving. The reporters were quiet. The whole room was eerily silent. Not even the computers were humming. No one was texting. *Be honest,* Hathaway reminded himself. He faced the crowd. Dennis moved a few feet away. He did not acknowledge her. He looked out and saw the cameras, the concerned expressions. They all knew something was wrong.

"I have an update," Hathaway started. The words caught in his throat. He swallowed and waited a few seconds for his thoughts to clear. The reporters waited. Then, he told them the truth.

CHAPTER 7

The ceiling show ended. Hathaway roused himself. None of the officials gathered in the conference room had said anything for a long time, immersed, as he was, in their thoughts and memories. He asked if they had heard the tape. They all had. There was no reason to play it again. Instead, they unanimously agreed to rename the Martian site after Arti and Kate, officially changing the basin's name to Katearti. Since no one was likely to return to the Red Planet, they suggested creating a memorial in Titusville, the home of NASA, similar to what was done for astronauts who had previously died. A small statue engraved with the names of the deceased astronauts had also been placed on the Moon. If anyone went there again, the statue could be updated.

Hilliard entered quietly.

"Was there a chance the aliens could somehow discern the source of the ship endlessly orbiting Mars?" Kelly asked. "If so, could they threaten Earth?"

Everyone turned to Dennis, who brightened in the spotlight. "It is possible," she said. "However, anyone would hesitate to attack an entire civilization. Any aliens would be millions of miles from their home base and supplies."

"That didn't stop Cortez," Kelly noted, referring to the Spanish assault on the Aztec empire. "Or Pizzaro," he added. "He took down the Incas."

"The conquistadors were a lot closer to Spain than an alien would be to its home planet," Dennis countered.

"Maybe they don't have a home planet," Kelly said, getting obviously antagonistic. "Maybe they are raiders who live in ships and travel around attacking planets."

"Maybe," Dennis said through clenched teeth. "Maybe they are a super race. Maybe they eat humans. Maybe they read science fiction books."

Hathaway held up his hand to quiet them. They glared across the table at each other. Hathaway had thought of the possibility aliens would trace the astronauts back to Earth but hadn't brought it up. He couldn't imagine how the feuding countries on this planet could ever work together to fight off invaders, particularly ones with superior weaponry. People in this small meeting couldn't even get along.

"Could our weapons defeat an alien force?" he asked, moving the conversation in a different direction. He listened as the others discussed the use of missiles before suggesting the matter might better be handled by someone trained in defense, such as the Joint Chiefs of Staff or the National Security Agency. Hathaway agreed. No one suggested having PAL play a role. Hathaway certainly didn't. He definitely didn't want Laarson involved. The guy was a genius bent on gaining as much publicity as possible. He was caught up in his imagined gunfights and was very unrealistic.

Checking his watch, Hathaway realized it had been almost two days since hearing from Kate. He felt only despair. Maybe what happened to her and Arti was a harbinger of the future of those on Earth. He stood up, signaling the end of the meeting. There was nothing more to do. Boeing could complete the second rocket, but it wasn't going anywhere. Laarson envisioned trips to some distant galaxy—the electromagnet rays would always be available for propulsion—but the distances were daunting. Sci-fi movies might show astronauts in suspended animation, but that technology didn't exist yet. With belligerent aliens in the picture, travel anywhere might be impossible.

Hathaway started to walk to the door when he saw Consuelo press his right hand to his ear. Hathaway stopped. Consuelo was maintaining contact with Mission Control, where staffers were still trying to re-establish communications with the Martian astronauts. Hathaway felt his pulse pick up. The others didn't notice: Hilliard and Kelly were whispering to each other while Collins and Simpson were nearing the door.

"Wait a moment," Hathaway called. Everyone stopped.

"We're getting something," Consuelo said. "There's some static," he added. "The module seems to have powered up."

"Lord," Hathaway said, barely able to breathe. Anxious faces turned to him. He sat down. Consuelo followed suit. The others did, too.

"Does that mean Kate is still alive?" Simpson asked.

"I don't know what it means," Hathaway answered. "Maybe the

aliens figured out how to fix the link." He could feel the eyes around the table boring into him. He put his earpiece back in. He could hear the static. Somehow, it felt like a strong signal, a sense of life amid the deep darkness of space.

"Mission Control is getting readouts. The computers are on," Consuelo said. "Readings are normal." He paused. "Nothing from Kate."

"Could the computers reactivate themselves?" Hilliard asked.

"Yes," Consuelo said. "They can self-correct under certain circumstances." Hathaway felt his stomach fall. Somehow, whatever was causing the blackouts fixed itself. Or someone or something did. Wouldn't Kate report in? Maybe she couldn't. Maybe turning on the module was all she could do. She might be trapped with just her small amount of food and no help within any distance.

He knew Mission Control was trying to raise her. The same thing happened when Apollo 13 returned to Earth after a near-disastrous explosion. Joe Kerwin kept trying to reach the three astronauts but only heard silence. Actually, the astronauts needed extra time to respond and finally did, much to everyone's relief. That was minutes. Kate hadn't been heard from for more than 40 hours.

"She's not answering," Consuelo said.

Hathaway sagged. He didn't have to say anything. The others understood. He turned up the sound in his earpiece. He listened to the uneven buzz, hoping to detect something amid the hum. The computers were alive. They were transmitting. Something human existed on that distant planet. After a few moments, he shrugged. A forlorn hope. He started to get up again. The others took one last sip of coffee.

"Colonel," someone said in Hathaway's ear. He needed a moment to recognize the voice. Kate. He straightened. A surge of energy spread down his back. He was sure his hair stood on end.

"Kate!" he cried, even though he knew she wouldn't hear him for 14 minutes. Coffee cups clattered to the table around the room.

"I am opening the door," Kate was saying. "I don't see any aliens. Everything is very quiet."

Hathaway couldn't help smiling. Kate! He breathed. He didn't care that she couldn't hear him. She was alive.

"Are you sure it's Kate?" Kelly asked.

Hathaway stared at the astronaut. Was Kelly suggesting aliens could imitate Kate's voice? They couldn't know how far away help might be. Hathaway dropped back into his chair. Was this a trap? Elation flooded away, leaving him drained. "I think so," he mumbled.

"It's her," Consuelo reported. "Voice patterns match."

"I can see poor Arti," Kate was saying. "I can't even bury him. Radiation… Never mind. There's not much left."

"How did she survive?" Kelly wondered aloud.

"I hope you can hear me," Kate said. "I haven't had any communication in hours. Thank God, MOM is still functioning."

"She must have stayed hidden," Hilliard said. "That's what I would have done."

Hathaway almost retorted to that claim but stopped himself. This was no time for any sarcasm.

"MOM is listing," Kate continued. "I am not sure I can lift off without a stable base."

Immediately, Hathaway tried to think of a solution. She could pile up dirt under the capsule and level the ground. How? One person couldn't do that alone. MOM weighed more than 2,000 lbs. even without a fuel load. Maybe Kate could try to take off. If she left Mars at an angle, she could correct enroute to Odin.

"Any ideas?" he asked Kelly, who shook his head.

"We don't know how much MOM is listing," Kelly responded. "Are there any images?"

"No video," Consuelo answered.

"Can MOM take off at an angle?" Hathaway tried.

"Maybe," Simpson offered.

Hathaway tried not to look disappointed. That was no help.

"I'm going to use Worm to get rocks under MOM and level her," Kate announced. She was panting. Hathaway grinned. Clever girl. "It sure is heavy without Arti to help," Kate continued.

He could hear her struggling and then the sound of Worm starting up. Would it work? Could she control the device? Hathaway held his breath. He could envision this brave young woman, millions of miles from safety, conjuring up solutions. His muscles tensed as if helping her. He could see the others in the room going through the same mental anguish.

"It worked," Kate cried a few minutes later.

Suddenly, the dark screen behind Hathaway lit up. Feeling the light, Hathaway turned in his seat. Kate's helmet cam showed MOM sitting evenly with rubble under one side. Worm extended toward the capsule.

Everyone applauded, clapping each other on the back, hugging.

Hathaway stayed apart. *Finally,* he thought. He felt such enormous relief. Kate was going to be able to get back to Odin and head for home. Consuelo was walking toward him. Hathaway fought back tears. They shook hands.

"She did it," Consuelo whispered, almost unable to express his emotions.

Hathaway nodded. There was nothing more to say.

CHAPTER 8

Mission Control never lost contact during Kate's long flight back to Earth. The computer glitches ceased and never returned. As a result, the whole world was riveted on her solo effort, comparing it to Lindberg's flight across the Atlantic or to Apollo 13's heroic return from the aborted trip to the Moon. Media ran out of superlatives while broadcasting continuous coverage across the four months. Her daily diet was analyzed; her exercise routine debated. Pundits offered pop psychological interpretations of her mood, while media seers predicted her mental and physical condition upon her return.

On Earth, various committees gathered to discuss how to honor Arti. They couldn't agree, breaking up into partisan groups based on ethnicity, religion and/or gender. The last idea Hathaway heard was to name an area north of Cape Canaveral "New Armenia" and put a statue of Arti there. Unfortunately, the residents north of Cape Canaveral were not consulted and promptly objected when the concept was broached on social media. The local state senator who promoted the suggestion then insisted he had never heard of such a ludicrous proposal.

Hathaway stayed clear of the ensuing arguments. Still somewhat overwhelmed by everything that was happening, he rarely left his office. He had a cot brought in and stayed in contact via his computer, grateful as the time lapse slowly declined. In the interim, he participated in endless interviews with breathless reporters who wanted to know his "true feelings" when he heard Kate's voice after such a long silence.

"Relief," he told them. "And pride. Kate was personally selected for this unprecedented flight." Of course, Kate's participation resulted from a group decision, but Hathaway had no qualms about accepting full credit. He did attend a ceremony in Bangladesh via online video where Kate's parents were honored for having such a wonderful daughter. Her father spoke a few words while her mother busied herself setting up dates with potential suitors.

Hathaway was pleased both parents seemed delighted by their daughter's success. At least the father stopped parading their son in front of TV cameras, and her mother accepted her daughter might be capable of making her own decisions now. "After all," she told a reporter from the *Protham Alo* newspaper, "she is flying back from Mars on her own. She only needed a man to get there."

Even better, Hathaway noted, Kate's brother was offered a job as an on-line marketer for a company selling car warranties. Hathaway considered starting an office pool to guess how long the brother held that job.

Mostly, Hathaway devoted his time to supervising the return flight, making sure everything was set for Kate's arrival. He did fend off questions about who should play him in the upcoming epic movie about the trip, although hearing one of the more handsome leading men was proposed was definitely an ego-boost. His wife discounted that idea, given the age disparity.

"He doesn't have to be my twin," Hathaway protested.

"Thank goodness," his wife said.

When the delay in communication finally disappeared, he and Kate had a long, private talk. She was exhausted and saddened but determined to complete her mission. She didn't feel the need for a counselor. Rather, she just wanted lots of time to rest. Laarson was already talking about a movie and a book. Kate said she'd think about it, but, to Hathaway, she sounded reluctant. Meanwhile, Laarson was marketing "space" drinks bearing Kate's name that supposedly gave her strength, along with dolls in her image and a variety of other tie-ins. His various companies were mass producing an endless supply of products while TV was running a long series of reconstructions that depicted the Martian events while running ads for the various tchotchkes.

In the NASA gift shop, Hathaway noted shelves crammed with every possible item bearing Kate's name, from ash trays to pennants. He found an entire area filled with alien dolls and miniature spaceships based on Kate's descriptions. Stores around the world were stocking similar keepsakes. Meanwhile debates raged throughout social media over whether Kate represented an important step for women by surviving or timidness by hiding while her brave male companion faced off against the aliens. Or was Arti fool-hearty in contrast with the calm and thoughtful Kate?

Meanwhile, the oft-ridiculed UFO fanatics were reveling in attention and making broad claims about past visits to Earth. They had a champion: Dr. Dennis was now the most-frequent guest on talk shows. Hathaway even read where some movie producer was planning a bio of her life. Her autobiography was already a best seller. Apparently, she wrote it prior to the Martian mission and simply updated it. In many countries, survivalists or "preppers" were busy furnishing underground shelters and stocking up in anticipation of the arrival of the murderous aliens. Worldwide, Laarson sold more than a million of those pre-packed units, all installed by one of his companies with food supplies included. His clients were in their glory, showing up in TV accounts and being the subject of detailed magazine articles about how to properly burrow underground.

On a more somber note, Arti's name was added to the plaque in the atrium in a small ceremony, while his official photograph now hung in the memorial portion of the Hall of Astronauts. "New Armenia" was no longer included in the discussion.

Hathaway participated in NASA remote meetings about future flights. As he expected, no official there thought a repeat mission was a good idea. He also attended online video sessions with the NSA and CIA about possible defense against an alien invasion. The Joint Chiefs of Staff were calling for massive spending on new weapons and revived a Reagan-era proposal that recommended orbiting weapons' platforms armed and ready to repel any invader. The plan had been dismissed back in the 1980s after millions were invested, and it was derided as "star wars." Now, it seemed the height of prudence.

In concert, television and theaters began replaying old movies like *Independence Day* and *Extinction* where humans eventually overcame terrible alien attacks. *Star Wars* and *Star Trek* were resuscitated with producers planning more prequels sequels. Several radio stations even broadcast Orson Welles' famed radio play based on the book *War of the Worlds* that depicted reports of a "real" invasion. As happened in 1938, a few people thought the report was accurate and properly panicked to the delight of reporters eager to demonstrate superiority by demeaning them.

Meanwhile, Kate continued her lonely trek across the solar system. The ship's technology made it possible for her to navigate alone, but the effort was stressful. Hathaway invited several psychologists to chat with her privately in the guise of NASA officials gathering information. They found her strong and seemingly unaffected by the trauma. She missed Arti, they said. However, since she harbored no romantic feelings toward him, she was able to handle his death with limited shock and sorrow. "She is amazingly composed," one told Hathaway.

Hathaway felt tremendous elation when Odin neared re-entry. He sat in his office, watching the picture of the big rocket now visible via satellite as it pierced Earth's atmosphere near the end of its 42-million-mile return flight. Kate was composed seated in the pilot's chair and even waved at the camera. If anything, her return to Cape Canaveral was almost anti-climactic. An experienced pilot, she guided the rocket to an easy landing at LZ-1, one of two sites built by SpaceX on an old launch complex.

Technicians helped her leave the ship. The sound of applause radiated almost around the world. Tears flowed. After changing into a suit designed to reduce the possibility of carrying any dangerous microbes, Kate met with doctors before going into the standard two-week quarantine and debriefing. Laarson bought a copy of the resulting tapes and commissioned a book about her experiences. Her parents spoke to her by phone. Her mother wanted to introduce her to a young man personally selected to be her husband. Kate pled exhaustion.

Hathaway let her rest for the mandatory two weeks before visiting her in her apartment. He brought along one of the popular dolls in her image. Kate found the acclaim humorous. She remained self-motivated and wanted to know about future assignments. Hathaway explained the alien presence doomed any future Martian adventures.

Kate disagreed. "We can handle them," she said. "I was just unprepared."

Hathaway didn't argue. Kate had survived and now looked back on the experience as exhilarating.

"There's also concern an alien army would follow you back to Earth," Hathaway noted.

Kate shook her head. "I doubt that," she said. "I watched the radar carefully. There was nothing."

Hathaway accepted that. He also knew Mission Control was monitoring the skies, too, and hadn't detected anything unusual. Still, NASA engineers were working on how Odin's radar was blocked by the aliens so equipment at the Cape couldn't pick up any signals. The same thing could be happening now. NORAD and other security agencies around the world maintained a steady vigil, scanning the skies constantly for any hint of an invading force. None had pinpointed anything, which only made officials more anxious.

Kate didn't mention Arti. When Hathaway expressed his sadness at his death, Kate nodded, but didn't say anything. Hathaway decided she must have been too preoccupied with her solo flight and was focused on the present, at least mentally. Hathaway decided Kate probably wanted to move on from her experience.

Once Kate emerged from isolation, she began a whirlwind tour of talk shows and media programs, repeating her account. NASA's Simpson accompanied her and monitored her activities. Hathaway watched at a distance, amazed how well Kate maintained her poise amid seemingly endless questions and demands on her time.

Laarson kept pushing her to do more. Hathaway protested quietly, noting that while Kate was still young, she needed to rest. "*Morgenstund har gull i munn,*" Laarson said. "As you say, 'the early bird gets the worm.'"

"Even birds need their rest," Hathaway countered.

"In a year, she will be forgotten," Laarson said. "She'll be teaching at some university. Her students will look at her and say, 'Was she someone once?' Who remembers Neil Armstrong, except in crossword puzzles and trivia games?"

"She's not a walking cash register," Hathaway protested.

"*Smi mens jernet er varmt,*" Laarson said.

Hathaway didn't need an explanation. Laarson used that phrase a lot, too: "strike while the iron is hot." He had another one in a similar vein: "*Å være midt i smørøyet.*"

"I'm thinking of Kate," Hathaway said. "I don't think she's in a good situation."

"*Hvor lite du vet,*" Laarson answered. "You know very little. But I know something. If there are no new Martian trips, you are unemployed."

Hathaway sat back in his chair. "I've thought of that," he said. "Maybe it's time for me to retire."

"With everything that is planned?" Laarson countered quickly. "We need you. We just have to find someone like Kate."

"There aren't many like her," Hathaway said. "Besides, no one should want to put anyone else through the harrowing experience she endured."

"*Man skal ikke skue hunden på hårene*," Laarson said softly.

Hathaway sat up. *Don't judge a book by its cover,* he repeated to himself. What did Laarson mean? What book? What cover? Was he implying Kate wasn't being honest? Or was there more going on that Hathaway didn't know? Or was Laarson just playing games, like he did with Hilliard? Fire her in public as part of a well-orchestrated move and then hire her. What could possibly be pre-arranged involving aliens? Laarson certainly didn't control them. What about Arti? How could Laarson have finagled that? The thought sickened Hathaway.

Laarson looked so smug. Hathaway let the various thoughts settle. There was no way even a trillionaire, millions of miles from Mars, was able to control the situation. What was he missing? Like the tape, something was hidden in plain sight.

"If you see something different, you should tell me," Hathaway finally said. He hesitated and then blurted, "*Å snakke rett fra leveren.*"

"Very good," Laarson said with a grin. "Speak directly from the liver. You have learned some Norwegian idioms." He turned away for a moment. Then, he stared at Hathaway as if formulating the words. "My English is still too poor," he finally said. "Maybe after a few more years, maybe I can explain." He exited the meeting.

Hathaway sat in his quiet office. Laarson's explanation could not be true. His English was very good. Norwegian children were introduced to English at an early age. They also bone up on the language through social media, music, TV shows and movies. Laarson's words gnawed at him.

He listened intently to the tape again. Kate was obviously scared. Arti was dead. An alien was approaching the module. Hathaway still could detect no false notes. He rationalized that exhaustion was clouding his thinking. He had a headache anyway. He was too old for puzzles. Who could he talk to? Consuelo? What could he add? Dennis? At least she was a woman. Maybe she had some insight.

He called her and tried to explain what Laarson said. She weighed the comments. "I don't think we were watching a video game," she mused aloud. "We know Odin really did fly to Mars with a two-man crew. We know Arti died there. The readouts from his suit make that very obvious."

Then what? Hathaway thought.

"I'll talk to her," Dennis offered. "She might have repressed some memories or been unwilling to talk about them."

"No," Hathaway said. "That's my job."

Dennis nodded. "I'm very busy anyway," she said before signing off. "I'm on the *Tonight Show* and then *Good Morning America*. I am also up for tenure."

Hathaway congratulated her, but his mind was elsewhere. What was he going to ask Kate? He didn't know. She certainly wasn't responsible for anything Laarson said. He liked to play games anyway. Hathaway stared at the wall with the pictures of his family. Was there more going on than he realized? Did Laarson have a secret agenda? That was possible. Hathaway regularly talked with the Norwegian inventor but their conversation rarely strayed from business updates. Still, considering Laarson's comments, there had to be some secret Hathaway wasn't privy to. What? Laarson was a businessman. That's all he cared about. Hathaway thought of all the souvenirs, the underground shelters, the pending movie. Could Laarson have been scheming to boost sales?

How could Hathaway find out? After a few more minutes of thought, he called Heidi Nielson at PAL. She popped up on the screen and smiled at him.

"You must be so happy to have Ms. Khatun back safely," she said.

"I am," Hathaway replied, "except I have to write a long report. In all the confusion, I've lost something I need. I hope you can help."

She nodded.

"I need copies of Pohl's directives to the astronauts," Hathaway said. He tried to sound matter-of-fact, hoping Nielson didn't realize he had no idea what Laarson may have told the astronauts privately. He may have said something. He certainly talked to them on several occasions while in training and prior to the launch.

Nielsen thought a moment. "I don't know," she started.

"I'm sure Pohl won't mind," Hathaway added quickly.

"That's not it," Nielsen said. "As I recall, he just wished them *lykke til*. That's Norwegian for good luck."

"Anything in writing?" Hathaway tried.

"Let me check the files."

"I'll wait," Hathaway said. "I just want to be complete in my report."

"Of course," Nielsen said.

Hathaway watched her type on her computer. She went to several sites. A serious older woman with gray in her hair, Nielsen studied each intently. Her brow furrowed. "Oh," she said. "Here's something." Hathaway waited. "Mr. Laarson wrote several notes to Ms. Khatun."

"None for Arti?"

"No."

"I'll go with whatever you have," Hathaway said. What could Laarson have told her? He definitely didn't provide any information about the launch or in-flight activities.

"I just emailed them to you," Nielsen reported. Hathaway thanked her and said goodbye.

He didn't open the files immediately. Instead, he mentally ran through the events. What did Kate do to help Laarson's businesses? Just going to Mars would have been enough. He couldn't have arranged for an alien attack. He couldn't have foreseen Arti would be killed. Hathaway had no idea.

Then, he opened the first file.

CHAPTER 9

Initially, Hathaway felt obligated to confront Laarson directly. He rehearsed several times, conjuring up Laarson's responses and countering them. He confided in his wife.

"I am coming home," he told her.

"For an hour?" she asked.

"For good," he answered.

"About time," Eva said. "You need to retire."

"You won't get sick of having me around the house?" he teased.

"Probably," she replied. "But maybe you could take up gardening."

To fortify himself, he listened to the Martian tape again. Maybe he should talk to Kate first, Hathaway thought. Laarson helped precipitate what happened. Kate probably wouldn't appreciate that. However, he didn't want her belligerently calling up Laarson. She might also go public. Hathaway didn't want that to happen before he spoke to Laarson. If anything, Laarson would simply retreat inside his research facility and let some hapless underlings get pelted in the spotlight. Besides, the public worshiped Laarson for his success in rescuing the planet from climate change and for his other inventions, one of which used electromagnetic rays to cure diseases. The scales of public opinion would always tilt in his direction.

Finally, two days later, he called Nielsen and asked to speak to Laarson. The young Norwegian popped onto the screen.

"What is up?" he asked without a hint of concern. "Have you found more astronauts for the next flight?"

"No," Hathaway said as calmly as possible. "I'm calling to tell you I am resigning and to tell you why." Hathaway noticed Laarson did not seem fazed by the statement.

"Again?" Laarson said. "You used the word retirement a few days ago."

"That was a suggestion," Hathaway replied. "This is a statement."

Laarson fiddled with a pen on his desk. "You read my note to Kate," he said. "Ms. Nielsen told me."

Hathaway expected that. Nielsen was a good secretary. "You

should have destroyed them," Hathaway said.

"Kate knew what I wrote her," Laarson said. "Besides, what is wrong? I was reminding her a space flight was more than a technological feat. It was an opportunity for business and could be exploited."

"Your English is suddenly very good," Hathaway noted.

"I continue to study," Laarson said. "The letters bothered you. *Hvorfor?* Why? Did you ever go into the NASA store? You can buy souvenirs. That's true at every football game, basketball game, tennis match. This is a business. We are making money by going to Mars."

Hathaway shook his head. His planned conversation was already off track. "When did Kate start shilling for PAL?"

"Shilling?"

"You know what it means," Hathaway snapped. "Was she pretending there were dots on the radar just to build ratings?"

"That is a good idea," Laarson said. "I am sure she saw aliens."

"How do you know?" Hathaway retorted. "Maybe she made that up, too? How can you separate truth from fiction?"

"You are upset," Laarson said.

"You are damn right," Hathaway said sharply. "I had no idea I was producing a damn TV show."

"That was not a set," Laarson said. "Odin really flew to Mars and back."

"Really?" Hathaway said. He abruptly closed the screen. He had never felt so angry. He couldn't sit, but got up and began to pace the office, getting more outraged with almost every step. He marched to his desk and demanded Hilliard be sent to his office.

"Sit down," he commanded when she arrived. She drew back but followed directions.

He leaned across his desk to face her. "Who told you the mission to Mars was only to exploit resources for PAL Industries?" he asked in a very cold, clipped voice.

"Laarson," she replied, straightening and smoothing her dress. "He came up with all those silly promotional ideas. I just presented them."

"You knew he would fire you?" Hathaway asked, aghast.

"Yes," Hilliard answered. "That was part of the deal. I think I played my part well. TV reporters really have to be actors. Laarson said I may get to play myself in the movie."

"In exchange, you got a job," Hathaway said, feeling light-headed. Hilliard seemed completely unconcerned.

"A very good job," Hilliard said.

Hathaway was bewildered. "How could you report such things on the air? How could you tell people things that were not true?"

Hilliard shrugged. "I worked for Warren News. No one believed me." She stood up. "Is there anything else?"

"I'm leaving," Hathaway managed. The words stuck in his throat. "I'm going home."

"It's a new world, John," Hilliard said. She stopped by the door with her hand on the knob. "Old guys like you get a pension. The rest of us adapt to reality."

Hathaway looked up at her. "What's reality?" he asked as the door closed.

He needed a few minutes to collect himself before activating his desk computer. Kate was holding a press conference in the media center. She remained calm as ever, talking in a clear voice without a quaver. Hathaway still admired her poise. He could barely listen to her recounting the events on Mars, answering questions. Behind him, his three monitors showed Kate. He flipped through channels. Every station seemingly had stopped regular programming to broadcast Kate's news conference, the latest in a series.

Studying the image, Hathaway realized the table placed in front of her podium had several items on it—a Kate doll, a T-shirt with the words "Welcome Home" and a model of the Odin rocket. Hilliard was standing to the side with a microphone at ready.

"What do you think happened to the aliens?" a reporter asked.

"I don't know," Kate answered. "I don't care. They left."

"Did the aliens try to get into the capsule?"

"I don't know that either," Kate said. "Maybe NASA can dust for fingerprints."

"Troy Commons, Warren News," a man said. Hathaway recognized him immediately. "Is it true there never were any aliens?" Commons demanded. Other reporters booed him.

Kate did not react beyond a wan smile. "I was there, Mr. Commons. You weren't."

Applause inundated her. Kate just smiled and waited for the tumult to calm. "If anyone should know about fake news, Mr. Commons, you would," she said, looking around and appearing smug as the next surge of applause and laughter died down. "Any more questions."

Hathaway could only watch for a few more minutes. Preferring quiet, he sat back in his chair and thought, absorbing everything around him, remembering. After a few moments enjoying the respite, he called Worthington in Alabama. *That should be my final task,* he thought. Worthington again apologized for not having the second rocket ready in time. It didn't matter, Hathaway assured him, thanking him and promising the next director would be told just how competent Worthington is.

"We're having trouble with the radiation shield," Worthington said. "I think we can get it solved by the time Mr. Laarson wants to send the next expedition."

After they said goodbye, Hathaway started to leave but stopped by the door. Radiation? That struck a chord. He sat down at his desk and played Kate's tape again. Then, he contacted Consuelo.

"How did NASA monitor radiation levels on Mars?" Hathaway asked.

"Two ways," Consuelo explained. "Instruments on Odin and MOM."

"Did both continue to operate while the astronauts were there?"

"Odin did, but MOM cut off. That's when all the instruments failed except the audio," Consuelo said.

Hathaway expected that answer. "Alien interference?" he tried.

"Probably," Consuelo said.

More like Kate couldn't access Odin's motherboard, Hathaway thought. "Send me Odin's radiation readouts during the time Kate was on Mars," he ordered.

"Roger."

They arrived within minutes via email. Hathaway didn't fool himself that he understood all the numbers, but he could see the peaks. As he suspected, radiation levels never topped 20 after the initial burst. He signed off and shut down the computer. Maybe someone would notice the discrepancy, but it wouldn't matter. Who was going to debunk a national hero? Especially someone like Kate, who always prepared far in advance. She would make a great business leader. That's probably what Laarson recognized.

He tried to imagine what happened. Maybe Arti hit on her. Was that what the wink was about? Did he expect her to surrender eventually? That wasn't Kate. She must have planned for that eventuality for a very long time. After a moment to calm himself, Hathaway dropped his beeper on the desk. The cell phone came from PAL Industries. He left it, too. He then took the family photos off the wall and put them in his briefcase. Then, he realized PAL also supplied the briefcase. He emptied it, placed it on his empty desk and hugged the pictures to his chest.

"I'm leaving," he told Wei on the way out.

"When should I say you'll be back," his secretary asked.

"Never," Hathaway replied. "Thank you for everything."

"What about the miners? The next flights to Mars?" Wei asked. "Who's going to oversee that?"

"Laarson will find someone," Hathaway said. "I have a garden to take care of."

He turned; pictures clasped tightly, and walked to the elevator. He could feel her watching him. He knew she would be calling Laarson as soon as the elevator door closed.

BOOK TWO:

YOUR MARTIAN TOURIST GUIDE

CHAPTER 1

Opening the foam door to the round observation platform, Cecil Townley was immediately disappointed to see no one had fixed the metallic "Welcome to Mars" sign. It still blazed red, but was tilted to the right, something he had dutifully reported to the maintenance committee weeks ago. *Someone should have responded and corrected the problem*, he thought. After all, he was the lone Martian tour guide, the sixth in his family in that role, and should carry some kind of clout.

Frustrated, he tried to push the sign into a level position. It didn't budge. He glared at it. This was the first thing visitors and new residents saw after leaving the airport and descending via one of the two elevators to the observation platform overlooking the colony carved three kilometers below the surface of the Red Planet. The elevator doors opened directly on the other side. One by one, tourists would step from the elevator car and, instead of being overwhelmed by the panorama clearly visible through the glass windows, Townley told himself, they would see that lopsided sign. What would they think of Mars then?

First impressions were very important, he repeated silently.

Next, he checked the cameras that surveyed the platform. Both were working; their green lights were all Townley needed to see. The cameras were actually dummies—the walls were wired to monitor everything going on, but the lights were green to indicate the recording was taking place. Martian executives some years ago thought residents needed some kind of indication everything they did was being scrutinized. Nevertheless, every inch of the circular area remained visible to the monitors in the control room. Not that there was ever a problem. Visitors were usually overwhelmed by the reality of being on Mars and having a chance to see the incredible man-made vista from this vantage point. If anything, the only concern was injury from jaws hitting the floor in amazement.

Continuing his routine, Townley slightly increased the audio. Typically kept at a low level when residents made the trip up to the observation deck so as to not overwhelm the senses, the music was amped up whenever a tourist group came by. A combination of whale voices combined with supposed cosmic sounds created by famed Martian musician Pompano Brisbane, the music provided the kind of eerie background visitors had come to expect. Centuries of science fiction presented in various media had conditioned everyone coming to the Red Planet to look forward to certain things, including Townley's blue jumpsuit as well as the atonal melodies that greeted them. The same music drifted throughout much of the city, providing the kind of backdrop anticipated by visitors and endured by residents.

After checking the chronogram embedded in his metallic tracking bracelet, nicknamed BID (bracelet ID), Townley paused in front of the mirror strategically placed in the corner. His hair was combed. His mustache was trimmed. His blue suit was crisp; his nametag shone in the overhead light. Even his identification bracelet somehow seemed smaller and less obtrusive. Every visitor asked about it, especially since it featured glowing amber lights. It's nothing, Townley would assure them. The government mandated such bracelets to ensure everyone remained healthy and protected. Residents could also be located immediately, guaranteeing crime was not a problem in Katarti.

Satisfied with his appearance, Townley completed his pre-tour activities by checking for any scraps of paper, even dust, that may have collected along the rim of the circular platform. He was discarding what little debris could be found into the waste tube when the elevator beeped. The machinery was silent, but engineers had added a small noise so Townley was not caught unawares by the arriving car. He glanced at his BID. The next group was early. That did happen occasionally, which is why he always arrived 30 minutes before any scheduled visit. Martian time, he called it. No one had schedules here, so arrivals and departures were somewhat haphazard.

While waiting for the door to open, Townley silently rehearsed his patter. Nothing could be left to chance. Some tourists were concerned about the radiation bombarding the planet. Others had heard about Mars quakes and asteroids. Townley always assured the nervous newcomers Martians knew the risks and were ready to depart whenever the planet became untenable. A host of ships remained at the ready for just such an emergency.

That was an easy concern to handle. Some of the questions,

however, were bizarre. In the past, one earnest woman tourist was sure Commander Khatun had an alien love child upon her return to Earth. Despite the passage of years, she read about it recently on a social media site. Another was convinced aliens had infiltrated Mars already and wanted to meet one. Then, there was one guy who was positive many residents of Mars had evolved into strange shapes and had been hidden away so as not to scare new arrivals. That was the result of some ancient and absurd Arnold Schwarzenegger movie set on Mars and still being shown because of its subject matter. The newest rumor circulating insisted Martians were unwillingly participating a nefarious scientific experiment to cultivate new organs for sick residents of Earth. Some of the twisted stories still resonated with Townley. He learned all of them, including the latest ones some tourist might try to surprise him with, and hoped he was ready with answers. He had to be.

After all, tourists expected him to know everything about Mars. That included not only obscure historical information, but also the most outrageous rumors and tantalizing gossip that was being talked about on Earth. He needed to know about it, and the tourists expected him have a solid answer or rebuttal to it—no matter how far-fetched it was.

The right elevator door softly slid open. Instead of awed visitors stepping from the car, Townley was stunned to see two uniformed policemen wrestling with a huge, thick-set, bearded man. The three combatants were sprawled across the elevator's floor, writhing, pulling at each other in a tangle of arms and legs. The man was screaming words like "End tyranny! Down with fascism! Freedom!" while, at the same time, trying to free himself from the cops, one of whom was vainly attempting to attach light handcuffs. While Townley had no idea who the man causing the ruckus was, the other two combatants were very familiar: Einar Mohr, who proudly wore the name of his Norwegian ancestor who helped build Katarti and now assisted in the observatory; and Sung-Ho Kim, the descendant of a Korean miner who could date his family back five Martian generations and volunteered at the greenhouse.

Neither was a cop, who were rarely seen anyway. Maybe, Townley thought, they were auxiliary police, members of a secret cadre of cops no one knew existed. Kim did have a radio transmitter attached to his shoulder. Only an official would do that, Townley decided. He made a mental note. Something to add to his know-ledge reservoir. His father never told him about such a private force. Perhaps the senate approved it in some kind of private vote. Townley made another note to read the official record again. Maybe this time he could stay awake.

At the moment, he was more concerned about the scene unfolding in front of him. Townley was astonished to see the two residents grappling with anyone. Martians rarely fought, not with all the controls and supervision. There was nothing to fight over: everything in the stores was free. No one needed a job; everyone volunteered and received credits that were used for extras, like an extra day at the spa. Automatons handled all the actual labor. Gov-ernment income came from sale of iron oxide used as colorants in various Earth products, such as cosmetics and magnetic ink, as well as the mining of lithium, cobalt, nickel, copper, zinc, niobium, molybdenum, lanthanum, europium, tungsten and gold.

"Stop struggling, Brown," Mohr ordered with little success. He held the shimmering handcuffs in his left hand while vainly trying to pinion Brown's formidable body. The big man continued to flail his arms and kick. Panting hard, Kim had taken hold of one massive leg and could barely stay on the floor. Townley thought Kim would be stomped at any moment.

Aghast, Townley wanted to do something, anything, but guides were trained to reconcile concerns and answer questions, not to tackle a bearded behemoth spitting angry words. His name may be Brown, Townley thought, but his manner was more red-hot anger. Brown's furious cries echoed around the observation platform and made Townley back up even further, continually checking that the cameras recorded everything happening.

He wasn't going to get very far anyway, Townley told himself, well aware that, like all visitors or residents, Brown wore a BID on his arm. It was broadcasting his presence and behavior back to the monitors. Facial recognition would complete the identification. With that hard evidence, Brown would have a hard time explaining his unwarranted behavior to the Commission before being perma-nently exiled back to Earth. *No one needed his kind up here*, Townley told himself fiercely. He would be glad to testify at some future hearing when Brown was securely restrained. At the moment, how-ever, he preferred not to get involved.

Kim's shoulder radio cackled. "Negative," Kim replied, gasping for breath as he continued to hold Brown's right leg. The big man tried to get up, but the weight of his two opponents was too much. He fell forward. He was still shouting slogans, but now his words were barely audible, tangled in his beard and smooshed by the hard flooring. He struggled to push himself up with his thick arms. He seemed like a giant beast raging against his captors. At first, his herculean effort didn't seem to be having any effect. Then, he staggered to his feet. To Townley's horror, with one massive kick, Brown sent Kim almost flying across the platform. He banged into the welcome sign with a hard thud.

Trying to remain out of the fray, Townley sidled toward the stricken gardener, who was sitting with his back to the sign. He reached out a hand. Kim waved him away. "I'm all right," he managed in a weak voice. Panting, he slowly stood, although needing to place his hand on the wall to remain upright.

Brown seemed surprised the impact hadn't slowed Kim. Hands on hips, almost in exasperation, he stopped and stared at him. Brown's great chest rose and fell with mighty breaths. To Townley, he resembled some kind of medieval, fire-breathing dragon, albeit one clad in denim overalls and a black turtleneck.

Rushing to take advantage of the momentary lapse, Mohr pinioned the giant's massive left arm and slammed the automatic cuffs on Brown's left wrist. They immediately locked and attached to the right wrist. Brown whirled, but was too late. He could no longer use his arms. In another moment, Mohr added light manacles around Brown's legs. The big man teetered and then toppled backwards, lying in the middle of the platform and writhing in frustration. His lack of mobility didn't silence him. Wild words accompanied by spit spewed around the room.

"You can stop me," Brown bellowed, "but freedom is coming."

Townley wanted to add, "Not for you," but restrained himself. Although not directly involved, he was breathing hard. His pulse had shot up. *Be calm,* he told himself, although the sight of Brown squirming on the floor was having the opposite effect.

For a moment, Brown quieted. The two volunteer cops sat down, panting and drained. Townley needed several large breaths to calm himself. "Good job, men," he finally said, nodding at Kim and Mohr. He felt enormous satisfaction the rebel had been subdued. Such episodes were becoming too common. This was the fourth in just the last month. All involving new arrivals, like Brown. They didn't know Martian ways and were seemingly unaware of the tight supervision despite in-flight briefings. Sadly, Townley thought, no one really listened enroute.

No one had entered the observation tower so violently. The previous protestors had waited until the political sector, where they had to be restrained by automatons before charging into the Hathaway Justice Center. They would have their hearing in a few weeks. No one understood what they were complaining about. Freedom? Townley sniffed at the thought. Martians were free; anyone with a lick of common sense would realize there had to be some restraints. Rules were necessary for anyone to survive in such a harsh environment. *Thank goodness,* Townley told himself silently, *some residents are trained and ready to handle such disruptions in the daily life of honest citizens.*

After another quick glance at the time, Townley realized the expected group of tourists was due in just a few minutes. He hoped the two auxiliaries could haul Brown off to custody before they arrived. His presence would definitely not provide the good first impression Townley cherished.

Now steady on his feet, Kim spoke clearly into his shoulder radio with several code words. Townley recognized them. He knew all the police codes as well as almost every other tiny detail of life on the planet. "Stand down," Kim was reporting. "All clear."

Definitely volunteer cops, Townley told himself. How many others served in that capacity? He would have to find out.

Townley watched proudly. The Martian safety forces were so adept. These two men, easily outweighed and definitely outmuscled, still managed to subdue a dangerous man. How Brown got this far was a mystery. He obviously managed to get through security and onto the elevator. *The Commission will have to plug that leak,* Townley thought. Not that it mattered. Brown could not have gone any farther without knowing the proper code to press into the keypad, and that was in the guide's bailiwick. The elevator wouldn't descend to the city without that input accompanied by visual recognition. No newcomer traveled this route without a guide.

"Whew," Mohr wheezed. Townley nodded appreciatively at the astronomer who, while still a bit winded, had enough energy to smile back.

Glaring at Brown to show his disdain, Townley surveyed him. Bearded, red-eyed with uncombed hair, he seemed the epitome of a revolutionary. They called themselves Fakers for no explained reason, and as far as Townley was concerned, they were well named, being completely delusionary. How many more of these people had to be arrested and exiled back to Earth before the nonsense about overthrowing the government ended?

Kim listened to something via the radio and gave Mohr a thumbs-up gesture. "We'll take it from here, Winny," Kim said to the dispatcher via the radio. To Townley's surprise and shock, the lights on the cameras suddenly shifted from green to red. While the cameras were dummies, the lights told viewers if the locale was being monitored. Suddenly, it wasn't.

Mohr also checked the cameras and then released the handcuffs. "You okay, Brownie?" he asked.

Getting to his feet, Brown rubbed his wrist. "I had no idea the darn things were so tight," he complained.

Townley stared. Something was definitely not right. Brown turned and looked at Townley. "That the guide?" he asked.

Mohr nodded. He wasn't smiling anymore.

Brown stared at Townley as if absorbing every detail of the guide's appearance, from the trim, blue jumpsuit to the short hair and dark glasses. Townley felt exposed by the hard glare. He glanced at the uniformed men; they seemed completely unfazed.

Townley felt the wall behind him and was grateful for the support. He wasn't sure what to do. Visitors generally stepped off the elevator in a good mood and were awestruck by the 360-degree view of the great city of Katarti stretching out around them. Standing exactly 500 meters above the red-adobe buildings, they could see the Laarson Sea in the distance, the experimental agricultural field, amusement park, business district, apartments and homes as well as the ribbony conveyor belt sidewalk transporting people around the various sectors of the Martian metropolis. They might even overlook the misaligned sign. They definitely didn't look at him with an obvious sinister grin. They also didn't stalk toward him with less than good intentions.

Inching away, Townley could feel the big man's towering presence. *Brownie indeed*, Townley thought He was more like the giant in

Jack and the Beanstalk. Brown stopped a meter in front of him and rubbed his massive hands together.

"Townley?" he asked. Behind him, the two cops watched. To Townley's dismay, neither seemed inclined to intervene.

Used to his usual spiel, Townley felt unable to ad lib anything. The music seemed to fade, overwhelmed by his pulse pounding in his ear. He gulped some air, trying to compose himself. Looking to his right, he could see the camera on that wall was still not working. The green light was off. He peeked to his left. That camera also had a red light. The Safety Department was still not monitoring the situation. The cavalry was not on its way, and the two volunteers who should have been protecting him seemed to have defected.

Brown grabbed Townley's arm. "You're coming with me," he ordered. Sweat poured down his face. All Townley could see were angry eyes and specks of saliva on the man's gray-brown beard.

"I'm not going anywhere," Townley said as firmly as he could. His voice quavered a little. Brown tightened his grip with his left hand. Townley felt as though his right arm had been placed in a vise. "Let me go," he insisted, trying to get away.

Brown shook his head. "Forget it," he growled.

"Don't fight it," Mohr told Townley. "They need you."

"They?" Townley squeaked.

"Admit it's red already," Kim interrupted with a Martian idiom, blocking his partner's next words. "Winnie can't keep the sky blue forever."

"What?" Brown asked in obvious exasperation. Townley didn't explain. Martians had developed their own slang and were in many ways beginning to move away from their home planet. For tourists, Townley would use the comparison of Australia to England, where accents and slang changed over the intervening centuries. He didn't mention that to Brown. The big man seemed upset enough already and seemingly devoid of a sense of humor. Kim was saying they should admit the obvious and hurry up.

"Who's Winnie?" Mohr asked.

"New recruit," Kim replied. "Just met him."

"He did a great job," Mohr said.

"None of this will do you any good," Townley interjected. "The cameras are everywhere. Security will be on to you any minute."

"You wish," Brown said.

Townley used his free arm to point at the closest camera. To his horror, the green light still had not returned. He managed to crane his neck to check the other camera. It, too, remained off.

"Let's go," Brown said. He urged the two cops toward the elevator.

"My back is sore," Kim moaned, stretching and rubbing it.

"My knees got pretty banged up," Mohr added.

"Sorry," Brown said. "It had to look real."

"It felt real," Kim said.

"I may need two massages," Mohr said, trying to touch his toes.

Townley felt sick to his stomach. What was going on? He glanced at Mohr. "Relax, Cecil," Mohr told him, using the proper English accent on the name. Townley hated it when his name was mispronounced. "No one wants to hurt you. They need you alive."

"For what?" Townley gasped.

"Brown," Mohr invited the bearded man.

"Not now," Kim said. "Papa Bear can't wait. You know how quickly things get repaired around here." He rushed to the elevator and pressed the down button. The right door opened. Muted music poured out.

"I can't go," Townley objected. "I have a tour group coming."

"Not anymore," Brown told him.

"I'll meet 'em," Kim said.

Townley stared at Kim in disgust. For close to 200 years, only a Townley had led guided tours of Mars. What did Kim know? Townley drew himself up. "I'm not missing my tour," he insisted.

"There's no time for this," Brown growled. He grabbed Townley's arm. Mohr took the other one. Together, they pulled Townley into the elevator. The metal door closed. Surrounded by the soft music to ease any tension visitors may feel and bathe them in the sounds of an alien world, Townley felt completely trapped, even though both men released their holds on his arms. The last things he saw on the platform were Kim, running a comb through his hair and flexing his right leg, and that the welcome sign somehow had been straightened when the amateur horticulturalist fell into it.

Brown nudged him toward the control. "We're going down," he commanded.

Townley felt sick to his stomach. What if he didn't tap in the correct code? He couldn't defend himself in this small room. Mohr was not going to be any help; that was clear. Worse, they were not being observed in here. The red light on the camera glistened. Townley clenched his fingers. He could prevent them from reaching Katarti, but at what cost? Brown would kill him. Townley was convinced of that. The big man's dark eyes shimmed with contempt, a sure indicator of homicide.

Inching toward the wall pad, Townley kept waiting for Mohr to intervene. The volunteer cop must have sworn to uphold Martian law. Every resident had to take that vow. Townley knew the oath well. So did Mohr and Kim, since they repeated it during Laarson Day ceremonies every March. Maybe this was some kind of trap, Townley thought. Mohr was playing along in order to capture the rebel leaders, the ones who sent Brown. That could be it. Townley felt invigorated. Sure, he told himself. All he had to do was follow instructions. No doubt the rest of the tiny police force or a legion of automatons were waiting on the ground floor for Brown. Convinced, Townley straightened.

He tapped his code into the keypad. The screen above it brightened. The face detector scanned him. Then, the elevator immediately revived and began a slow descent. Watching through the glass exterior as the city grew closer, Townley tried to figure out a way to communicate with Mohr, hoping to alert him the plan had been recognized. He could see the volunteer cop's reflection in the glass and made an elaborate wink. Mohr, however, was checking his sore wrist and didn't notice.

Brown did. "Allergy?" he asked. "I get eye irritation all the time." He reached into his pocket and pulled out a small vial. He offered one to Townley, who declined. "They're just Vitamin C pills with an antihistamine," Brown explained genially. Again, Townley waved the offer away. "Suit yourself," Brown said. "My grandma swore by them."

As the elevator continued to drop, Townley felt a little stronger. It would be over soon, he told himself. No doubt, he'd be stuck for a while supplying an official statement. Someone would have to call Betsy. His wife might panic if he didn't return on his usual punctual schedule. And what about his son, Cecil VII? Feeling much better, Townley weighed taking some action. He was no hero. His father often chided him for being so inoffensive. On the other hand, didn't

Commander Artsruni take on murderous aliens with just a flashlight, albeit unsuccessfully? Didn't Commander Khatun somehow elude an alien fleet on her harrowing four-month flight back to Earth? With such examples, Townley steeled himself, how could he hesitate?

He gave a sideways glance toward Mohr. The handcuffs hung from his belt. Mohr was not paying attention. Townley inched a little in the astronomer's direction. All he had to do was grab the cuffs and slap them on Brown. Maybe Mohr was coerced into cooperating. As soon as Townley made his move, Mohr was bound to help. Townley readied himself. Mohr would appreciate the assistance, Townley thought, and Cecil V would be impressed. Cecil VII certainly would be.

Brown shifted a little, causing Townley to pause. He imagined himself taking the needed two steps to get to the handcuffs, grabbing them and turning to face Brown. The big man would have felt Townley move. He would be staring directly at Townley and probably not very happy. Townley considered that. Brown had a powerful kick, which he had demonstrated in the observation deck fight. He was calm now, but, if Townley took hold of the cuffs, the burly giant might revert to his ferocious state. Townley realized there was no way to escape, at least not here, surrounded by glass and slowly descending to the ground. The security forces had to be waiting there. Or, he thought, looking through the window at the city slowly expanding as the elevator continued downward, if he was wrong about Mohr's plan, he had a better chance of eluding Brown when they reached Katarti. He could easily find a place of refuge, and they'd never locate him again—until Brown's trial and expulsion.

As the elevator continued to complete the final kilometers to the ground, Mohr took a BID from his uniform pants and put it on Brown's wrist, replacing the one that had been there. The old one was stuffed into his pocket. He then carefully punched in a code on Brown's BID. Green lights encircled the bracelet and then turned amber. Mohr then held Townley's arm, punched in a code on his BID. "All set," he said.

Townley stared at his bracelet. What had Mohr done? Townley studied his BID. The two embedded lights glowed yellow. And he immediately realized what Mohr had accomplished. The BID was sending out a false locale.

"Where are you?"

"Home," Mohr said.

"Where am I?" Townley asked.

"On the platform," Mohr said. "Giving your tour."

Townley did not reply. *How had the bracelet been rigged? Why? What are they planning to do with me?* Townley glumly glanced at his captors, completely puzzled. Nothing like this ever happened on Mars, where society was carefully ordered to allow humans to live in such a harsh, inhospitable environment. Checking his watch, he felt panic increasing inside him as the time for the tour group grew closer. That feeling overwhelmed him once, years ago, when as a young tour guide, he had been seconds from missing the elevator and the incoming visitors. His father had given him a stern lecture, and it had never happened again. Until now. Could Kim pull off the charade? If not, Kim wouldn't be hurt but Townley's reputation would be shot. Rather than handcuff Brown, he wanted to go back up to the observation deck and perform his duties.

Brown patted Townley's shoulder. "You are on the ground floor of a new Mars," he said. "We will soon be taking over,"

"We?" Townley quavered.

"The FKR," Mohr interjected. "Free Katarti Rebellion." He smiled at Townley. "You know the best part?" he asked. Townley shook his head in puzzlement. "You are going to be our guide," Mohr told him triumphantly.

CHAPTER 2

"Look natural," Brown whispered as the elevator door slid open to reveal the entry platform. From here, every visitor would be able to enjoy the amazing view of a spectacularly red underground city stretching out in front of them—not some distant mirage seen from above but very close and very real. Brisbane's music sifting through loudspeakers added to the other worldly sense. To Townley, even after so many trips up and down the elevator, the sights and sounds always enchanted him. Until today.

Instead of admiring the people passing on the moving sidewalk or standing by the many red-adobe buildings—all three stories or less—that stretched away from the elevator, Townley looked for any evidence of police and realized, to his dismay, no one was awaiting them. Instead, there was just the music, welling around them and drifting across the active community.

Townley was dismayed and felt his spirits sag. Not even the music could buoy his emotions. Somehow, he had not been able to shake the idea of an immediate rescue. Clearly, he and his kidnappers were not being greeted by a security welcoming committee. As far as he could tell, everything looked completely normal and placid. Since no one had to work, residents often went to the entertainment sector where holographic performers staged continuous programs, to the sports sector for nonstop games or the beach. Some took classes at one of the two colleges; others exercised, volunteered or simply chatted with friends. They didn't anticipate crimes or get involved.

For a moment, in desperation, Townley focused on a small queue of Martians waiting to use the elevator to ascend to the observation platform—a common hobby—or to continue onto the departure gates to return to Earth. There were always a few, unable to cope with the restrained lifestyle and distance, who wanted to leave Mars and fly back to their homeland. He could see a man and a woman with suitcases.

How could he alert any of them? Townley tried to catch their attention, even though his right arm could not escape Brown's grip.

He stared. He blinked rapidly. Nothing. The departing couple seemed lost in thought. The other dozen or so people there were intent on getting into the elevator. They paid no attention to Townley and his companions. He wanted to yell, but they could see a uniformed security officer with him. They wouldn't do anything. No one interfered with the police, even one who was not official. Besides, other than Townley, few Martians kept tabs on residents beyond their immediate circle of friends. Gossip was invariably boring. There was no reason to talk about someone else with the constant monitoring.

The music soared, flooding the streets and open air. No one said anything or complained.

For a moment, Townley considered using his cell phone, but hesitated. Such a move would be extremely obvious and likely provoke an angry reaction from Brown. He felt the cell phone press against his leg as if urging him to use it. He glanced around. Mohr was keeping close tabs on him. There was no way to pull out the phone. He waited while the others stepped onto the moving sidewalk—locally known as the Caterpillar—that rolled in front of the elevator and continued around the districts. Maybe, if he fell behind, he could punch the emergency code into his phone. He tried to stop, but Mohr wouldn't let him. He grabbed Townley's left arm. Townley looked around, hoping someone saw how Mohr seized his arm. No one did. Passersby seemed absorbed in the music and their own thoughts.

A few people idling across the street seemed the best option, Townley decided. They were close enough to provide some assistance if he tried to fight back. However, they continued to ignore Townley and his two companions. One was reading a book; another was studying his cell phone. Two were chatting. Townley was hopeful one of them would spot the danger or sense a problem. They obviously didn't notice anything amiss and concluded Townley was leading another tourist group. In their mind, the visitors would not be staying. Mars had reached its capacity of 8,000 residents; those hoping to relocate would have to wait until some of the older residents passed on and were cremated in the core of the planet, becoming one with this alien world.

"Act like you are giving a tour," Mohr hissed, as they all climbed onto the moving sidewalk. It rolled flat to the ground, making entrance and exit extremely simple. It rarely stopped, even for someone who was disabled. Special platforms coordinated to the speed of the Caterpillar served as an entry for residents who were physically limited.

"A tour?" Townley hissed. Feeling emboldened, he snapped, "Take your shoes away from that door."

Brown turned. "Huh?' he muttered.

"Martian idiom," Townley explained. "It means that's not going to happen. You couldn't have turned off all the cameras. The real police" —he nodded sarcastically at Mohr— "will see what's going on."

Mohr leaned over. "They'll see me," he whispered. "In my uniform, I am a very persuasive illusion."

"How long do you think you can keep this up?" Townley asked, still talking in a low voice. He had no idea what Brown would do if the others on the sidewalk became aware something was wrong, but the man was strong and seemed capable of a violent response. No private citizen on Mars had guns, so a big man could inflict a lot of damage before help arrived.

"Uniforms are powerful weapons," Mohr replied. "I kind of like it. Not as useful as overalls, but darn attractive, wouldn't you say?"

"No," Townley retorted.

"Focus," Mohr advised calmly, nodding at other passengers and waving to an imaginary friend at one of the stores.

"What's with that music?" Brown interrupted. "It sounds like someone is playing a saw."

"That's one of the instruments," Townley told him. "You can also hear a fife, toha, cimbalom and a friction harp."

"What? No one can afford a fiddle?" Brown snorted.

"You can get partial symphonic music in Einstein," Townley told him. "The music changes a little depending on the section."

"This is?" Brown asked.

"PAL District," Townley answered automatically. "The shopping district. There's an outdoor mall and a variety of businesses." He paused. "The music is supposed to put you in a buying mood. You can pick up souvenirs of your visit. Haven't you been here before?"

Brown shook his head. "That's why I need you," he said.

Townley felt a little better. FKR needed him. Good. They

would not harm him. Until. He would have to drag out the process as long as possible. Security would figure out what was happening soon enough.

"Let's start the tour here," Townley said loudly. The others on the moving platform didn't bother to pretend to listen. Townley was too well known; at least his blue jumpsuit was. No one wanted to hear the same information they had been exposed to multiple times since their arrival.

"Good thinking," Mohr said.

"The city comes from the names of the first two astronauts," Townley started. "Aadya 'Kate' Khatun, who returned home safely in one of the most heroic flights in history; and Hamza 'Arti' Artsruni, who died during the original expedition to Mars. He was killed by aliens, which is why Mars has such elaborate defense systems and multiple available ships in case the aliens return. So far, the show of force has dissuaded any repeat attacks."

He pointed to the north. "A memorial to Lt. Commander Artsruni is located in the science district, which is named New Armenia in his honor," he said. "It is one of eight districts. We have an education district called Einstein, where you will find two colleges. Public schools exist in both residential districts, Eastland and Westland. I live in Westland. The residential areas count as one district. Another district dedicated to sports is named for Marwin Juffnagel, the top athlete in Martian history. There is a stadium and an arena there. Last year, the U.S. Olympic Soccer Team came here for an exhibition." His companions did not seem impressed. Townley continued the spiel: "The shopping district I already told you about. The political district hosts the newspaper and other media along with the senate chambers but is still unnamed since no one can agree on a proper title. Most people call it HA for 'hot air.'"

Townley waited to see if someone laughed. The political sector was actually called Hathaway, which was often shortened. However, his joke didn't resonate with this group. He quickly explained the correct name and emphasized the executive officers were there and the Commission met there to hear cases and determine if someone should be exiled.

"Exiled?" Brown asked.

"Sent back to Earth," Townley explained. "There are a variety of reasons anyone could be exiled, including committing a crime, such as," he paused for emphasis, "kidnapping."

Brown laughed. "That's something else we are going to change," he said. "Keep talking."

"There's the beach district, named for Bettina Hilliard, who was an important source of information during the first Martian expeditions," Townley continued. "Finally, there's the historic area with a museum, art galleries and several restored homes of the original miners. It's named for Troy Commons, a man who was once one of the most famous news reporters on Earth."

Brown obviously was not listening. "I want to know how anyone gets around all the electronics," he said in a low voice.

"Interesting question," Townley answered. That was his standard response even for the dumbest queries.

"Look," Brown said, leaning so close to Townley his beard brushed the guide's head. "You are here because you supposedly know everything about this place. You know the ins and outs. Right?" Townley nodded. "Then you know where we can avoid surveillance. Right?"

Townley took a deep breath. "There are no cameras in private homes," he said.

"But everyone entering or exiting is recorded," Mohr added. Brown gestured to him for a conference.

Townley looked at them, waiting for some decision. They were whispering to each other. He kept looking for a security officer. However, spotting one was almost impossible. All residents of Katarti knew the rules, so few were needed. The only weapons on Mars were the defensive Denny guns strategically placed on the surface along with atomic satellites ever waiting and ready for an alien invasion. One was always expected. Because of the strict statutes, most first proposed by the sainted founder Pohl Andre Laarson, the Martian court dealt with extremely rare civil concerns under the steady gaze of an impartial automaton judge. Besides, anyone violating the rules faced expulsion and a return to Earth, a fate all true Martians detested. Automatons, appearing completely human, existed everywhere, running businesses and handling all routine tasks. They also served as cops at the spaceport to greet newcomers, who expected to see uniformed security. Members of the tiny police force, then, were rarely seen and were invariably in plainclothes.

In fact, as Townley realized to his disappointment, Mohr's uniform caused others on the moving sidewalk to inch further away, giving less opportunity to ask for help discretely.

"We could go to your house," Mohr suggested to Townley

"My wife. My son," the guide gasped.

"They're not in the volcano," Mohr said. Brown looked puzzled. "The central core. It's hot," Mohr explained.

"Around fifteen hundred K," Townley said immediately regretting his reflex addition of correct information.

Brown cracked his knuckles as if emphasizing the point. Townley felt his stomach drop at the sound. "We needed to make sure you would cooperate," Mohr said. "We can always send them down the tube."

"If you do anything to them…" Townley started. He left the threat incomplete since, at the moment, he didn't know what he would do. Report them? That was pretty much all he could do. It seemed like a meaningless promise in the face of a dire threat. His shoulders sagged.

"That's up to you," Mohr said.

Brown grinned at Townley, who was feeling increasingly weak. "You will help," Brown insisted.

Townley gave a wan smile. "Do I have a choice?" he quavered.

Brown pulled his shirt from his pants to reveal what looked like a small gun in his waistband. "What do you think?" he asked.

CHAPTER 3

"Can't this thing go faster?" Brown asked, driving his heel into the moving sidewalk.

"It's set at two point two kilometers an hour," Townley automatically recited. "Most people walk around four point eight kilometers an hour, but the Caterpillar is designed…"

"Shut up," Brown interrupted. He did not look happy, looking around. "C'mon," he ordered and stepped onto the stone street. "No cars, right?"

"Just emergency vehicles, like an ambulance," Townley said. "They run on electromagnetic rays…"

"I don't need the entire encyclopedia," Brown interrupted. "He's like a little robot. Punch in a topic and stuff comes spewing out," he complained.

Townley didn't say anything. A good guide let an unhappy tourist vent. Brown could still be tired from the long flight to Mars and the subsequent wrestling match or mentally exhausted by the differences in weight, culture and even language, not to mention the commission of a crime. *Revolutionaries*, Townley thought, *such killjoys*.

As always, other people were riding the Caterpillar up and down the street. A few crossed from one side to the other. No one stayed long on the crushed stone. Townley glanced around, feeling exposed by walking on the road. That was unusual. On the other hand, he mused, maybe by being so obvious, security forces might be alerted. After all, they were trained to notice anomalies. What could be odder than three men marching down the main PAL sector street? On the other hand, Townley realized he did take tour groups into streets on occasion so the participants could get a better perspective. He just didn't keep them there.

He looked down the row of identical red adobe buildings in the PAL District, differentiated only by signage. If there were any security members about, they were well disguised. Of course, the street, like every inch of Katarti, was covered by cameras, but, Townley realized, monitors would only notice the tour guide with a two-man troupe.

"Nice weather today," Brown said, apparently trying to make normal conversation. He glanced around as if someone might be listening to his words.

Townley couldn't help but smile. Martians did not talk about the weather, which was the same every day. Fluffy 3-D clouds rolled overhead against a vast ceiling painted blue for effect. The structure blocked radiation; it didn't enhance storms. The effect appeared real, although residents soon saw the artifice behind the illusion. Townley held up a wet finger as if checking the wind.

"It doesn't look like rain," he told Brown.

Mohr stifled a laugh and tried to look away so Brown couldn't see his grin.

"I think you're right," Brown said seriously. "How often does it rain?"

Townley hesitated. He really didn't want to say "never." Water vapor rising as a result of human respiration was directed by fans to vents by the small experimental farm near the Laarson Sea. There it rained, adding to the filtered seawater used for irrigation. So far, the extra moisture had not helped. Little was grown there yet, although a lot of manure and fertilizers had been shipped in, since the Martian soil was not conducive to plant growth with its abundance of silicon dioxide and ferric oxide along with aluminum, calcium and sulfur oxides. As a result, Martians talked about lots of things, but weather was never part of the conversation.

Brown glanced at him, expecting an answer.

"Hardly ever," Townley finally said. "Mars is pretty dry."

Brown nodded and then seemed to become angry. Townley almost stopped walking. Had he said something wrong? He instantly recognized mood changes, a necessary skill since not all tourists responded well to an answer. Still, he was not sure what was wrong.

"Hurry up," Brown suddenly urged. He picked up the pace while staring to his right. "Someone is watching us."

"I see him, too," Mohr said. He almost began to run, yanking Townley along with him. The guide tried to slow him down. Had security finally realized what was happening? He couldn't see anyone. Then, by the edge of a pharmacy, he saw some movement. A head peeked around the corner. He immediately recognized Kim. The farmer edged forward and then sprinted across the street to join them. Panting, he fell in beside Brown. "They know," he reported. "I had to break off the tour."

"Oh," Townley moaned. His reputation was ruined. The tourists would tell others; he was sure of that. Tours on Mars were short and poor, they would say. That notoriety was worse than being forced to join this group.

"Winny kept the cameras off as long as he could, but Papa Bear rebooted," Kim continued. "The BIDs may be working again." Mohr immediately pressed a button on his bracelet to indicate a malfunction. He did the same to Brown. Townley noted Kim wasn't even wearing a BID. He was stunned. Didn't security recognize that?

Totally confused, Townley tried to focus on what Mohr had said. He had no idea who Winny was, but Papa Bear was local slang for the computer that oversaw all life support functions on Mars. Townley wondered if the reboot meant the monitors had been misled but would now see Townley hadn't met the tour group. They had to realize he was being held against his will. Inspired, Townley tried to work out some sort of signal to alert the monitors. After a moment, he put his hands behind his back as if they were pinioned there. He only had a brief second before Brown grabbed his left arm and propelled him forward.

"We got to get outta here," Brown said. He picked up the pace, plowing by another of the reddish adobe buildings. The others followed suit. Soon, they were hurrying into the Hathaway Sector. The buildings were the same—structural material on Mars was limited—but designs varied to match function. Brown kept looking back and then huffing on. His thick legs pounded into the crushed stone road. Townley had to sprint to keep up. His efforts to delay Brown were completely overpowered by Mohr's hold on his arm. Townley wanted to suggest they couldn't outrun a camera but had to sprint along with the others at Mohr's urging. If anything, he felt like he was in the grip of a tornado.

"I thought we were going to my house," Townley gasped at Mohr.

"Plans change," Mohr responded.

Brown finally stopped on a street outside a building identified by its sign as The Martian Planitia. Several people were going into the building. One, munching on some kind of cake, stopped to survey the quartet then shrugged and went inside. Bent over and panting, Brown eyed the building. "What's that?" he asked suspiciously.

"The newspaper," Townley answered. "It comes every morning via computer."

"Filled with fake news, no doubt," Brown snorted. He gestured at a small, square building just a few meters south of the newspaper office. "What's that?"

"The Warren Media Center," Townley replied before the cops could. "It's used for media conferences and government announcements. Nothing is scheduled today." He always checked the agenda. Tourists were always excited to see the Martian president or any of the district executives. Townley would have to explain there were no elections: leaders were selected at random by computers and served a maximum of two years. He doubted Brown was interested in that tidbit.

"Can we go there?" Brown managed. He was struggling to get his breath and had slowed his pace to a near crawl. However, he didn't release Townley, whose arm ached as badly as his lungs.

"Perfect," Mohr gasped.

They struggled up to the front door and inside. It was empty and unlocked. Brown seemed ready to ram the door when it slid open as he neared. No one locked anything on Mars, Townley could have told Brown, because of the ever-watchful cameras. Mohr guarded the door, keeping it ajar with his foot and surveying the outside, while the others tried to catch their breaths.

Panting, Townley realized leisurely walking on occasional tours was not keeping him in shape. Betsy kept reminding him to go to the gym, but he always found an excuse not to. Now, his lungs burning from just a short run, he conceded she may have a point. On the other hand, Brown was red-faced and wheezing while Kim looked ready to collapse. Mohr was standing, his chest heaving and sweat pouring down his face.

Seeing how spent they were, Townley began to wonder if, just maybe, if he could escape. Despite his own exhaustion, he didn't seem as incapacitated as the others by the gallop to the media center. Slowly, trying to appear nonchalant, he began to edge toward the raised dais and the door behind it.

"There must be six or seven security guys out there," Mohr wheezed, stepping away from the entrance. The door slid shut. Abruptly the music stopped. "I don't think the arrest schtick will work this time. They have us on camera running together."

"Shut up," Brown snapped. His heavy words hung in the air. He pulled out a small cell phone and punched in a code. "Roger," he said after a brief exchange of information. "We need fifteen minutes," he told the others.

"Get rid of that," Mohr cried, pointing at Brown's phone. "They can trace you through that."

Brown dropped the phone as if it were suddenly hot. "How?" he asked.

Kim grabbed it and hurried to the side wall. He pulled open a metallic door and dropped the phone inside. "The volcano will take care of it," he said.

Brown looked at Townley for an explanation. "All waste is sent to the central core via ceramic channels. They are everywhere: homes, streets, buildings," Townley told him. "The volcano refers to Mars' center, which is cooling. So everything is fuel for the natural furnace there."

Nodding, Brown turned back to the others. "Wish we had something like that on Earth," he said. No one asked what he wanted to dispose of, but the comment had an ominous sound. Townley thought of his wife and son. Mohr had threatened to send them down the tube. Feeling a surge of adrenalin at that thought, Townley felt motivated to act. He had to escape. He had to save his family.

Although frightened and surrounded, Townley continued to inch away. Now breathing normally, he kept watching the others carefully. They were still recovering from the recent exertion. Brown sprawled over a chair, head back, chest heaving, arms and legs spread out like a giant spider. Kim, too, sat down and stared at the ground. He seemed incapable of moving far or fast. Mohr was studying the exterior via a front window. In contrast, Townley held his breath in fear of alerting his captors. They ignored him, lost in their own attempts to recover.

He felt behind and found a metallic chair. By now, he estimated, he had maneuvered 6 meters away from the small group and reached the front row of computer desks. The silent computers looked up at him. He sidled slowly down the row, acting as if he were tidying up by sliding chairs against the desks. He could hear his movements echo off the walls but could not muffle them. At the same time, he heard a deep rumble under the concrete flooring in the area between the stage and the desks. He had no idea what it was. Mars quake? They were uncommon but lasted longer than on Earth because the Martian crust was so dry and broken. Buildings were all reinforced with extra thick walls to prevent excessive damage.

The big fear was a quake could shift the ground enough to damage the covering dome's foundations, creating cracks that allowed lethal radiation to seep through. To Townley, the sky seemed blue as usual with no hint of any cracking.

Nevertheless, Townley felt panic rise inside him. It was inbred, the result of constant parental warnings about the danger of a quake. He didn't want to be inside during a tremor. The ceiling may hold, but the buildings were comprised of weak materials. He looked up. The building's ceiling was not shaking. The quake seemed confined to the area below the building. Maybe that would distract his captors. They didn't seem to be tracking him or aware of the noise in the ground.

Encouraged, he began to sidle farther down the aisle. If he could reach the end, he could then sprint to the back door. No one would chase him outside. He kept watching Brown. He was the ringleader. The big man was still sprawled out. *Just a few meters more*, Townley told himself. He could see the door. He could almost hear it slide open, feel the rush of air and the wild shouts erupting behind him. Grimly, he continued snail-like down the aisle.

Just before he cleared the last computer, the large, overhead screen behind the podium suddenly sprang to life with a face. Townley immediately recognized Arch Larchmont, the newly chosen head of Mars' Security and Defense. Townley was thrilled. Now the men who forced him here would get it. He turned triumphantly to face them as they whirled to look at the screen.

"What did you do?" Brown demanded, glaring at Townley. Before the tour guide could answer, Larchmont interrupted.

"I suggest you blame yourself, Mr. Cantrell," he said in a very officious manner, emphasized by his dark desk and piercing stare. "Mr. Mohr and Mr. Kim, you will report to the judicial building for an immediate explanation of your actions."

"I'm sorry, sir, but we cannot," Mohr answered.

Larchmont didn't seem concerned. "We can discuss the matter at your hearing before expulsion," he said calmly. "Why are you wearing uniforms?"

"Costume party," Mohr replied. "We are getting ready for Laarson Day." Kim just blanched.

"Mr. Townley," Larchmont began.

"I was kidnapped," Townley cried. "They did it," he said, pointing dramatically at the other three. Larchmont did not change expressions.

"I am disappointed in your actions," he said.

"I was forced to go with them," Townley insisted. He almost felt like crying.

"Perhaps," Larchmont said with obvious disinterest. Townley felt his hopes deflate.

"Gentlemen," Larchmont said, "if you are planning to stay a while, you might discover some leftover sandwiches from the conference last week, but I would not be overly optimistic you'll find much edible on the premises. Media appetites are powerful, especially when free food is involved." He smiled. "If you remain there a few more hours, you can attend the conference announcing your upcoming hearings."

"We did not come here looking for food." Brown said, shaking a fist at Larchmont's image. "We want freedom."

"You shall have it," Larchmont replied, clasping his hands together in front of him as if praying. "On Earth, you will be as free as you wish. We will not limit you in any way. Of course, I cannot speak for authorities on Earth."

"How many men do you got?" Brown snarled. "We're ready."

"Mr. Cantrell," Larchmont said, "I am sorry to disappoint you, but there will not be a fight."

"I don't believe you," Brown said. "That's a lie. We saw all these people watching us."

"You did attract attention. Not many people run on Mars," Larchmont said. "We prefer a more leisurely pace. Besides, we really don't need security. There's not much to do except to help old ladies get onto the Caterpillar."

"Sure," Brown sneered. "We know what's going on: the secret labs, the political prisoners."

"Ah," Larchmont sighed, sounding more like the exasperated school aide he usually was than a security chief. "I have no idea what you are talking about."

"Freedom!" Brown shouted. "We are here to destroy your

regime."

"We?" Larchmont asked. "There are four of you."

"Three," Townley shouted. He pointed one by one at the others.

"A lot more will be coming over to our side," Mohr insisted. "You can't hold us here."

"I don't intend to," Larchmont said. "You are free to go. However, I should remind you everything is being filmed. You cannot go anywhere in our small city without being identified. Just look at the corners of the media room." They all did. Cameras were focused on them. Each had a green light beaming, something Townley gratefully noted. No one had turned them off. With that evidence, he hoped to prove he was forced to join this conspiracy.

Brown walked over to the closest camera. He reached up and yanked it off the wall. It splintered on the tile flooring. Townley didn't say anything. Of course, the physical cameras did nothing but convince onlookers they were being watched. The walls did all the work here, too.

"That one won't be much help anymore," Brown snorted. "Besides," he told Larchmont, "I don't believe anything you say."

"We must worship at a different church," Larchmont said as the screen darkened.

"Was he right?" Brown demanded of Townley, who abruptly realized escape was not a possibility. "We can just leave?"

Since Brown looked so angry, Townley really didn't want to say anything. "If he says so," he began.

"It's a trap," Brown decided. "If we walk outside, we'll be gunned down."

"No one on Mars has any weapons," Townley said.

Mohr and Kim nodded.

"Then there's private security, like secret police," Brown decided.

"I have never heard of that," Townley said.

"More fake news," Brown responded. "You must think I'm really stupid."

"How are we getting out?" Kim interrupted.

"Working on it," Brown said. "We can't go back the way we came. But there's one direction outside of camera range." He checked his watch. "We have another four minutes or so." He then, one by one, jerked the other three cameras off their pedestals. Each slammed into the tile with enough force to fracture into multiple pieces. Their green lights continued to glow. To Townley, their destruction was amusing. The green lights testified the walls were still recording, and there was nothing Brown could do about that. The delicious part: he didn't know it.

Time oozed. No one said anything. Townley continued to weigh escape routes. However, considering Larchmont's distain, he was going to have a hard time proving his innocence. To think he went to the observation tower in such a good mood just a short time ago. Townley was getting angry over the turn of events and increasingly frustrated. He would need time to explain to Larchmont. Everything would be all right. It had to be. Why did the computer pick Larchmont? Why not someone with a little more understanding? Educators were a hard lot. They had heard a bevy of excuses over the years and rejected all of them.

Then something bumped against the floor by the front row of desks, maybe 3 meters from Townley. A moment later, the head and upper body of a man poked through the fractured tile. Dirt obscured his features, but he had a broad grin.

"Green," Brown exclaimed.

"More of a blueish-grey," Green replied, wiping some of the grime off his face and looking at it. "The red stuff doesn't go very deep."

Despite the dirty face, Townley recognized Green as a newcomer from maybe a year before. That was when a spate of deaths among the elderly residents opened up some available space. His name wasn't Green then either. However, Townley couldn't remember what Green's full name was, but the last name was Roberts. He also noticed Green wasn't wearing a BID. He couldn't do that above ground. He would be stopped immediately. Or not, Townley thought. No one had stopped Kim. Who would arrest Green? His mind reeled. He barely heard Brown urge them to go to the hole in the floor.

Townley couldn't move. He kept eyeing the rear door, but didn't have either the energy or the will to try. At this point, he realized escape was not possible. He slumped into a chair in front of a blank computer screen.

Mohr saw him and hurried to him. Townley watched as Mohr removed his own BID and flung it to the side where it landed in a heap of camera parts. He took off Townley's and tossed it against the side wall. As Brown strode by, Townley realized the big man's BID was already discarded. Townley gaped in amazement. The lack of weight on his wrist added to his disorientation. He felt almost naked.

"This is the fun part," Brown said, taking Townley's arm and almost lifting him from the chair.

"I'm not enjoying it," Townley replied as Mohr dragged him to the opening in the floor. Brown and Kim were already peering into the dark hole.

"I thought you liked jokes," Mohr told him.

Townley looked over the edge of what looked like a deep abyss. "I am not going into the volcano," he said, his voice quavering.

"Neither am I," Mohr said.

Brown dropped down and landed with a thud. Kim followed. "Your turn," Mohr told Townley. The guide hesitated. "You might as well," Mohr said. "You heard Larchmont. If you aren't with us, you're gone."

Still, Townley hesitated. He couldn't even imagine himself jumping into the hole, even with Brown raising his arms as if ready to catch him. "You are asking me to swallow a spaceship," Townley quavered, using a Martian idiom.

"Maybe two," Mohr said. "Bon appétit."

Townley felt Mohr move to the side. Then, he felt two hands on his back and was shoved forward. For a moment, he teetered and then, fell feet first. Trying, but failing, to grab on to the side of the hole, he landed on solid ground in less than a second. Standing, he could see Brown and Kim headed down what seemed to be a narrow tunnel. Mohr thumped to the ground behind Townley.

"Start walking," Mohr nudged him. "There are no cameras where we are going."

Townley could only see Brown and Kim in front of him, groping along the walls. He could smell the sulfur in the soil and see the line of red like a snake marking the break between the topsoil and the level of the tunnel. Air was warm and limited. Something was making loud noises. Each oomph sent a breeze into the corridor. Townley stumbled along, not knowing where he was going and positive it was some place he did not want to be.

CHAPTER 4

After a shower in a small bathroom, Townley felt a little better and walked into the large atrium. Since his blue jumpsuit was unable to endure the constant rubbing against the narrow tunnel walls, Townley was given some new clothing. Feeling out of uniform, Townley reluctantly accepted a collar-less shirt and simple stretch pants. They apparently belonged to a heavier man because they bagged, adding to his discomfort and embarrassment. A tour guide had to look professional. He was the first Martian any tourist talked to. Appearance was incredibly important. If he met newcomers dressed in billowing clothes, they would think he was a clown. Silently, he mourned the collapse of everything he knew.

Inside the large domed room, he glanced around, getting his bearings. From what he could see, this central atrium was connected by tunnels headed in multiple directions. The walls contained various chests and two large, built-in bureaus. A huge fan kept the air circulating. Green had used a hefty Worm to carve out a new pathway from the media center.

Townley sniffed. The smell of sulfur saturated the air. It had been weakened by the introduction of some kind of perfume, but the rotten egg scent still was quite evident. For Townley, the odor was both familiar and welcome. Everything else seemed out of place.

He did notice the terrorists' ingenuity. Given the scarcity of water, Martians relied on a dry vacuum system. Green, or someone who worked with him, had hooked one up and connected it to a ceramic tube leading into the bowels of Mars. They also tapped into the Laarson Sea to create a shower, rerouting the runoff back into the Laarson Sea. Nevertheless, Townley was sure enough Martian dirt remained in his hair to create a flower bed.

The other men ignored him. Townley didn't bother to conjure up an escape route. He would be lost amid the many tunnels. Instead, he just sat down and waited for whatever was to come next.

The quartet gathered around a flat table, apparently looking at a map. The wall beyond them featured a large console with multiple dials and readouts. Except for Brown, they were all dressed in new outfits. Mohr and Kim had removed their uniforms and replaced them with grey sweatpants and sweatshirts. Brown could barely fit inside the tunnel, so his clothes had been almost shredded by the constant contact. Somehow, he had found another pair of denim pants and a black turtleneck. He hadn't bothered to clean his face, which was smudged. Green, however, was more interested in appearance and had found a dress shirt to match his dark slacks.

Townley noted immediately all of their new clothes fit. Obviously, they had prepared. Couldn't they have stockpiled some appropriate clothes for him? He had many more blue jumpsuits in his closet. He would have been happy to have given them one before they kidnapped him.

Glumly resting in a plastic chair against the side wall, Townley distracted himself from his sad thoughts by looking around. Maybe he could remember enough to help authorities locate this place. Somehow, he noted, the FKR had managed to create a good-sized chamber under Katarti. They didn't have much choice, he figured. They couldn't survive outside the city, as rebels in Earth locales did, simply because there was no food or water in the unsettled Martian land still under the roof. As a result, the city's boundaries extended maybe 50 meters beyond the last buildings. Few ventured into the Deadland, as it was called, except as a kind of brief adventure. It was easy to get lost there, although the BID ensured everyone eventually returned safely. There was nothing to see anyway.

"Feel all right?" Mohr asked, wandering over.

"Not really," Townley said. "I'd like to talk to my wife."

Mohr glanced at Green, who shook his head. "Sorry. No connections down here."

Townley turned away. Betsy would be so worried. What had they done with her? He pulled out his cell phone. Mohr was right. There was no reception.

"Hungry?" Mohr tried.

Townley shook his head. He had not thought about food for a while. His stomach ached anyway from the stress.

"We have some great freeze-dried salmon," Mohr offered. Townley just waved him away. He was more interested in the conversation from across the room.

"I think our first target should be the computer," Brown said, pointing at the map.

"Big Papa," Kim threw in.

Townley preferred not to use nicknames, but didn't correct Kim. Feeling lost and filled with disappointment, he nevertheless forced himself to eavesdrop on the discussion. Maybe he could thwart the group's sinister plans. He just had to contact authorities. That would clear his name at the same time.

"I want to get those cells," Green said. "I suspect they are being held near the Hathaway Building. That's the political center of Katarti." He jabbed a finger at some point on the map. "We are in the correct sector."

"If we can sabotage the computer," Brown argued, "we can ruin the security. After that, we can liberate the political prisoners."

"In case security gets too nosy, we have bombs planted all over the city," Green said. "If we get cornered…kaboom!"

"Kaboom anyway," Brown said. Townley was appalled at how eager the big man looked to set off explosives. "If we don't get cooperation, we'll bring the whole place down with us. That's the Fakers motto."

The others raised their hands with fingers pressed together and touched each other in what Townley took as some kind of solidarity pledge.

Green considered the idea. "Only as a last resort," he finally said. "We can use the bombs as a threat if we get into the central office without being detected."

"That's where our tour guide comes in," Brown said. They all looked at Townley. "He knows every inch of this place."

Townley blinked. "Political prisoners?" he said, obviously puzzled. "I have never heard of any."

Brown gave a short, harsh laugh. "Look what we got? A shill for the government. I'm sorry we brought you along. You don't know anything. It's those stupid BIDs. They hypnotized you." He glared at Mohr. "Couldn't you have found someone who knew something?" he barked.

"There's only one tourist guide," Mohr shrugged.

"A piss-poor one, if you ask me," Brown snapped.

Townley almost protested, but didn't respond. What good would it do to say anything? he asked himself. Brown was stuck with him. Townley glanced about. Electromagnetic rays obviously cut through the Martian soil. These guys may think they were out of sight, but they weren't. They could be detected. Townley almost laughed aloud. He felt so much better. Someone was no doubt tracing them right now.

"After that," Brown continued, tracing a line with his finger, "I want to destroy the scientific experiments on young kids. That really gets me upset," he said, glaring at Townley. "Bet you didn't know they are using young kids as sex slaves and sources of DNA for medical treatments."

"No," Townley said weakly.

"Yeah, right," Brown said, rolling his eyes. "Then I want to get Laarson," he continued. "He's lived long enough."

"Pohl Andre Laarson?" Townley quavered.

"Who else?" Green asked.

"He's been dead for a hundred and forty years," Townley protested. Vainly, he looked at Mohr and Kim for some support, but neither reacted.

"He's a vampire," Brown said. "Geez, how did we get such an ignorant tour guide?"

Townley lapsed into silence. He watched the others carefully examining the map of Katarti. *They have to be crazy*, he thought. *Vampires? Sex slaves? Why would anyone believe such things?* He wouldn't mind if some of these ideas were bandied about in some kind of comedy show, but these men were serious. Where did they hear these wild tales? He doubted any of them were creative enough to come up with such absurd claims on their own. He wanted to ask; but didn't. Instead, he strained to hear sounds of someone coming to arrest them. Someone had to.

To his surprise and delight, he heard a noise down one of the tunnels. The others did, too. Immediately, Green opened a file drawer in a built-in bureau and produced several guns He quickly handed them out. Townley did not receive one nor did Green even hint he would get one. Not that it mattered. He was shocked to see the weapons. He knew Brown had one. Maybe a weapon could be smuggled in, but how did these guys get so many past security? No one was permitted to possess any kind of weapon on Mars, not even the police. He glanced down the tunnel in the direction of the noise.

Were security forces finally going to show up? He waited anxiously, moving to place himself partly behind the large desk holding a map. When the shooting started, he would be protected. The others fanned out around the room, guns pointed, while remaining half hidden by chairs. Mohr was in the bathroom, peering out through a crack, while Kim took refuge in the closet. His small gun swallowed up by his massive hand, Brown was too big to hide himself, so he backed up to a wall as if the curvature of the room would shield him. Green stood closest to the tunnel entrance. He held a finger to his lips. The room quieted, except for the fans. There was no music, something Townley acutely missed.

Townley tried to work out a scenario. He would immediately surrender. He would show empty hands to prove he wasn't armed. If the security team wanted, he could produce the torn tourist uniform, which he had kept. Green wanted to burn it, but Townley lied and said anything sent down to the volcano was recorded. Someone would see the uniform, Townley claimed, and believe the worst. His demise would be reported, causing a citywide alarm. Townley was so grateful Green accepted that explanation.

The footsteps were getting louder. Whoever was coming was making a surprisingly lot of noise. A scout? Townley wondered. Maybe some resident who stumbled over the tunnel and was exploring. An android? That was possible. One was sent ahead while the rest of the security force waited behind. Townley hung his hopes on that idea.

"FKR," a voice rang out.

Green relaxed. "It's Winfield," he said. The others immediately emerged. Townley stayed behind the desk. He had no idea who Winfield was, but was sure his arrival was not positive.

A few seconds later, a tall man strode into the atrium. They all greeted him. Townley didn't recognize him. Not a recent tourist or newcomer. Disappointed, he wandered back to his chair and slumped into it. *Someone,* he told himself, *is going to get a long and detailed complaint letter.* If that didn't work, he silently vowed, someone was definitely going to hear about these tunnels and the lack of action by the security forces. He would take it to Larchmont or the new president Evan Longstreet. Townley consoled himself with an image of marching into Longstreet's office and demanding action. Longstreet would be shocked to hear how little was being done to protect citizens. Townley was sure of that.

"Everything went great," Winfield said after shaking hands and clapping the others on the back. "I got clean away. Papa Bear never had any idea. With just a couple of keystrokes, I took out the entire camera system." That revelation brought more cheers and congratulations. "When Papa Bear rebooted, I got out and headed here."

"Were you followed?" Green asked.

Winfield shook his head. "I don't think so," he said. "I know they got some androids that can track someone anywhere, but no one was on my tail."

Damn, Townley thought.

"Good timing," Green said. "We're off to take out Papa Bear."

Winfield shook his head. "Tough order," he noted. "Security is tough. I'm told Papa Bear is protected by an army of automatons with razors for hands."

Townley perked up. Maybe that tidbit would end this foolishness. He could see consternation on the faces of the men in the room. They were reconsidering their options. While Townley had never heard about the robotic army, he didn't hesitate to chime in. "I could have told you that," he said.

"Why didn't you?" Mohr demanded, confronting him.

"I am not exactly here because I want to be," Townley shot back. "Better you find out some things for yourself." He stood as tall as possible with his hands on his hips.

Brown pointed a gun at him. Townley quivered but forced himself to stay defiant. "Any more surprises we need to know about?" Brown asked coldly.

"Maybe," Townley said. "I like surprises."

His face contorted in anger; Brown started toward him. Mohr grabbed Brown's arm. "We need him," he said. Brown dragged him for a few centimeters before stopping.

"For what?" Brown said.

Townley felt Brown's harsh stare. "I know how to get around the obstacles," he quavered.

Brown glared. "Let go of me," he told Mohr and pulled his arm away.

Mohr edged by Townley. "You're halfway to the volcano," he whispered.

Townley felt a cold chill. He could see the distrust, even anger, in the eyes surveying him. Even worse, he didn't know a thing about any defense around Papa Bear and even less about how to evade them. Maybe the Fakers would back out in time. He hoped so. He could just imagine being caught unarmed in some kind of crossfire. At the moment, though, being slightly wounded seemed like a fine option. The hospitals on Mars were excellent, manned by skilled automatons with human overseers checking the readouts.

On top of everything else, Townley was becoming increasingly upset by his lack of knowledge. That was the one thing he prided himself on: he knew everything about the Martian colony. Instead, increasingly, he was finding gaps in his supposed encyclopedic expertise. That was even worse than being kidnapped, he decided.

"Let's go," Brown growled.

The others nodded. "We've come too far to back out now," Mohr said. The others nodded.

Townley would have admired their courage if he didn't feel an overwhelming sense of impending disaster. He fell into place behind Mohr. Kim stayed right behind him, sometimes nudging Townley with his gun. "Keep up," Kim kept saying. "Don't get any ideas."

Ideas, Townley thought. At the moment, that was all he had. Facts were becoming increasingly hard to find.

Green took the lead with Brown bringing up the rear. Townley immediately noticed this tunnel was larger with sealed side walls. Air tubes lined the ceiling. Clearly, Townley decided, people had been working on this rebellion for some time. No longer stunned by such revelations, he began to wonder why colony leaders hadn't detected the tunnels. No one seemed to have noticed anything. That both disgusted and frustrated him. No wonder no one responded to his complaint regarding the crooked welcome sign. No one was tending to anything. Big talk, no action, Townley told himself.

Walking along on the hard-packed red soil, he could hear the mechanical pumps keeping the air moving. None of the familiar music permeated this deep, but lights marked the path at regular intervals, creating bouts of shadows. The sides had been smoothed. He ran a hand along the left wall. Someone had gone to great effort to remove the rough edges. Trying to get his bearings, he could see concrete footprints of buildings pressing down against the tunnel ceiling. He could not distinguish the sector or identify the structures. Down here, everything looked the same. He tried to measure distance based on his steps, starting with the media center: 5 meters, 10 meters, 20 meters.

Abruptly, Green stopped. "The Hathaway Judicial Building is maybe ten meters ahead of us," he whispered. "Keep your voices down. They have voice-detection equipment."

Townley almost objected. He had never heard of such equipment being used on Mars. He was sure Green was wrong, but was he? Was this something else Townley knew nothing about? He berated himself: how could he give tours and know so little? How many people had he lied to? The anguish engulfed him. Maybe there were hidden labs doing awful things. Maybe there were experiments being done on children. He hoped not. Political prisoners? There weren't even political parties on Mars. On the other hand, as he considered everything he didn't know, there may be secret parties as well.

He began to feel very dizzy.

"Tell me about the Hathaway," Brown interrupted Townley's reverie. The guide looked up to see Brown towering over him.

"It's three stories high with staff offices on the first floor. Council chambers are on the second floor," Townley recited mechanically. "Council meets twice a year for two weeks each. Members are chosen at random by the computer."

"What's on the third floor?" Brown asked.

"The monitoring devices as well as the mainframe," Townley said even though he didn't want to tell Brown that. The giant and his men could really crimp activities on Mars by yanking a few cords or typing in some devious code. He tried to muffle the words, but they all caught the implication.

"Papa Bear's lair," Winfield breathed.

Brown considered that. He turned to Green. "That's our target," he said.

Green walked over to Townley. "You go first," he ordered. "No one will think twice seeing a familiar tourist guide."

Townley gulped. Green was right. Townley often visited Hathaway, looking for information, schedules and names of new officials. The number of tours had declined recently as Martian officials tried to reduce the stress on food supplies. Regular shipments still continued from Earth, but the failure thus far of the farming efforts had curtailed expansion plans and strained food distribution. Tourists always asked about food, well aware Mars could supply little on its own. To be prepared for such tourist questions, Townley often dropped by the Hathaway Building to read official reports or talk to some of the politicians. Even the automatonic secretaries recognized Townley now.

"I'm not wearing my uniform," Townley protested. How could anyone tell he was the tourist guide without his blue jumpsuit?

"You wear one all the time?" Mohr asked.

"When I give tours," Townley answered.

"This is one time you aren't," Brown said coldly.

Townley looked down at his clothes. He would never go outside dressed like this. What was he going to do? He tried to picture the next events. He would leave the tunnel first. That was something. He didn't have to wait for the others. He could run into an office. Once separated from this band of misfits, he could seek safety.

Green seemed to read his mind. He leaned over and whispered in Townley's ear. "Don't think about making a break for it," he said. "We still have Betsy and your kid."

Townley nodded dumbly. Maybe he could call Betsy once he was outside the Fakers' control. His cell phone would work at ground level. More importantly, he would be clearly visible to the monitors. They would see his strange clothing. They could tell he was the only one not armed. They would have to realize he was being coerced into cooperating. He would never help the FKR. Why should he? He earned lots of extra credits for his tours. If he joined the Fakers, Betsy would lose her weekly pampering at the spa. Cecil would no longer have all the extra toys that so impressed his friends. No, Townley told himself, he would stay the course on behalf of his family.

Buoyed by that idea, he moved through the small group to the front. A metal ladder nailed into the wall awaited him. He looked up to see a shiny cover over a round exit. Where would he emerge? Wouldn't someone notice people popping out of a hole in the ground? Mohr nudged him; he grasped the metal rung and climbed up the 10 rungs. With each step, the ladder seemed to shift. For a moment, he wondered if his weight would pull the ladder from the wall. He hurried as fast as he could.

At the top, he could shift the metallic cover to the side. Immediately, he heard familiar music. He emerged on the side of the Hathaway Judicial Center, a red, sandy stretch of soil between buildings. To his right was the Laarson Courthouse. The media center was probably 50 meters behind him.

"Hurry up," Mohr called behind him.

Townley slowly pulled himself up and moved to the side as Mohr and Green quickly followed. This small alleyway was empty. Townley could see people riding by on the Caterpillar. No one looked at the men emerging from the ground. Townley spotted cameras on the edges of the buildings. The cameras were moving independently, scanning the area. Their green lights shone in the artificial sunlight. Townley thought about waving but restrained himself. The last thing he wanted to do was look happy. He frowned and acted as though he were about to cry as Kim clamored out and then Winfield.

"Happy to be above ground?" Kim asked him. "I'm not fond of this subterranean stuff either."

"I'd be a lot happier anywhere else," Townley answered.

Behind him, Brown was struggling to fit through the opening. He was seemingly stuck about chest high. At first, he pressed his hands against the ground, throwing up red dust like a flare. That effort accomplished nothing except to dust him with red speckles. He held up his arms so Green and Winfield could each take an arm and try to pull Brown from the hole. They yanked unequally. Brown yelled in pain and freed himself from their grasp.

He began to swivel, apparently trying to unscrew himself. More dirt fell around him until he seemed swallowed by a good-sized dust bunny. Despite the concentrated effort, he remained wedged into place. After a few minutes, he had to rest while the red dust settled around him.

Townley looked at Kim. "You're smart," he said. "How did you get involved with this lot?"

Kim turned serious. "I saw no choice," he said. "When I heard what was going on, I was appalled. Mind control. Did you realize the government is shooting rays at us that are designed to completely destroy our self will."

Townley was startled by Kim's fierce expression. The words were almost spat out. "Are you sure?" Townley asked. "Why would they do that?"

"Power," Kim said. "That's all it is."

Brown resumed his efforts. His contortions had created a few millimeters of space. Slowly, he freed his upper chest. His beard was now rust colored; his face, completely smudged with dark eyes peering out in anger. To Townley, it looked like Mars was giving birth to a very large offspring. From Brown's strained appearance, Townley thought they might need to carve a wider hole.

Townley looked at Kim. "You and your family, like mine, have been here for multiple generations. I've never heard anything about mind control. Did you ask your dad? I bet it would be news to him, too," he argued. "Why wait some one hundred and eighty years before doing it?"

"It doesn't matter," Kim said fiercely. "They are doing it now. They must be stopped."

With a loud pop, Brown was suddenly freed. He exited the hole and lay down, collecting himself while Green returned the cover to its rightful place. He then spread some of the red soil over it.

"Let's go," he said.

Brown slowly got to his feet. "I've got to lose some weight," he muttered. His shirt was creased around his middle as if someone had tried to fold him in half.

CHAPTER 5

The group began walking down the alleyway to the front of the building. Townley checked constantly to be sure the cameras had green lights. There would be no hiding now. This dangerous quintet was fully exposed. Townley couldn't wait for the hearings. How would Brown, Green and the others possibly justify their actions? They were on their way to Earth with every step they took here, Townley told himself. In the interim, he would just play along. In some ways, he was actually enjoying himself. *Think of it as a play*, he told himself.

Maybe, Townley thought, *acting might be a nice diversion when not leading a tour. The Mighty Martian Merrymen are always looking for new members.*

The front door to the Hathaway Judicial Center slid open. Townley was shooed inside first. The others followed, almost huddling together like a long train behind Townley's back. They quickly realized no one in any of the offices on both sides of the first floor were paying them the slightest attention. Townley could see automatonic secretaries and staff at work, rigidly focused on the task at hand.

The small group moved around the lobby, peering in offices.

"Some security," Brown loudly scoffed.

"There's nothing to protect here," Mohr pointed out. "These are just bureaucrats." He checked a secretary walking by with a small computer tablet in her hand. "Mechanical and efficient."

"Don't you think they'll alert the third floor?" Kim asked.

Green shrugged. "Probably," he said. "But that's where we have to go."

"No stairs," Brown noted after checking beside the offices.

"No bathrooms either," Townley said. "Killer automatons don't use the john."

"Over there," Mohr said, pointing at the elevator, which was nestled between two offices.

They walked over to it. Townley pressed three. He hung back when the door opened, hoping the others would step inside the car, leaving him free to run away. Instead, Mohr took his arm and propelled him inside. They rode up to the third floor while discussing how to handle the security forces no doubt waiting for them.

"Don't shoot right away," Green cautioned. "The automatons aren't programmed to fire."

"Remember the razors," Winfield added. He was sweating. Standing in front, Brown tucked his turtleneck into his overalls and seemed ready to charge into whatever awaited. Mohr and Kim were using the big man as a shield.

"Let Cecil go first," Mohr suggested. "They'll think we are a tour group."

Townley shook his head. "I've never led a group up here," he said. They all turned to look at him.

"Aha," Brown said.

"It's not like that," Townley said. "Papa Bear is well protected. I wouldn't think of challenging his robotic guards. They are elite, programmed to kill. I wouldn't go near them." He glanced around. Were they buying his story? Would they go back down?

"We'll get through," Brown said grimly. He hunched over, almost resembling a giant wrecking ball ready to strike. Mohr and Green raised their guns. Kim slipped to the back of the elevator, peering over everyone's shoulder. Townley stood to the side by the controls.

The elevator stopped. Townley could feel the tension in the small room. Slowly the metallic door slid open. Brown pressed back, hiding behind the door. He nodded at Townley. Mohr took the guide's arm. "Go ahead," he whispered.

Townley paled. Walk into the central control room? He couldn't imagine doing that. The guards would fire. They were probably aiming right now. He couldn't see anyone but only could see a few centimeters in front of the elevator. He felt Mohr give him a push. The pseudo-cop was staying behind Brown and remained hidden by the metallic end of the door and Brown's massive body. He nudged Townley again.

Timidly, hands raised, Townley stepped from the elevator and stood for a moment inside an almost empty room. He slowly lowered his arms, as if the wood panel were dangerous. Townley didn't see anyone at first. Instead, he just heard music. "It's all safe," he managed.

With a cry, Brown rushed out, gun ready.

"Oh," a voice squeaked. A small man with white hair, sitting behind a built-in stone desk, a wall of equipment and a small black box with dials, glanced at them and then began to gather several sheets of paper. A couple of sheets floated in the air, caught by the air from the overhead vent. The man gave up trying to collect them. He emitted another "oh," and hastily turned off the music. He picked up what looked like a small rod from a small collection of strange implements.

"He's armed," Green yelled. He fired. His beam hit the rod, splintering it. The man dropped it and stepped back.

"Stop," he cried. "You just destroyed my wood fife." He bent over the remains now lying on the floor. "Do you know how expensive these things are?"

No one said anything.

"Look," the man said. "I know I shouldn't be here now. I'll go quietly." He continued gathering the sheets of paper lying about and holding them to his chest.

"What is this?" Brown muttered. He started walking around, staring at the blank, paneled walls. He pushed against a ceramic panel. Nothing happened.

"Please," the man started and then suddenly straightened. "Townley?" he said and broke into a broad smile. "I thought you guys were the secret police." He put the papers back on the desk.

"See?" Brown said.

Townley started to walk toward the man and stopped. That voice was so familiar. He couldn't place it. So was the face. It took a moment: Palermo Brisbane, the musician. They shook hands.

"You guys had me going there," Brisbane said. "I like the acoustics in here." He gulped. "I know this place is off limits, like Deadland, but I can't resist."

"We are on a tour," Brown rumbled. His voice seemed to echo in the nearly empty room. He pulled the gun from under his shirt. It had been crushed by his body in the tunnel exit. He stared at it, vainly tried the trigger and then sourly stuffed the battered weapon back into his waistband.

Townley looked around. "I thought there would be lots of people here," he said. "You know, monitoring."

Brisbane chuckled. "Just me," he said. "How are you, Mr.

Townley?"

Townley gasped. It couldn't be. He closed his eyes, trying to focus on the sound. "Larchmont," he cried.

Brisbane nodded. "Very good," he said. "You have a good ear for voices."

Almost staggering, Townley tried to steady himself. "He's Larchmont," he told the others. They all looked at Brisbane and then at Townley and back at the musician.

"Naw," Brown finally said. "He don't look a thing like that guy on the screen."

Brisbane grinned. "Come with me," he said and invited them to his simple desk and the computer. He leaned over and typed something on his computer and pressed a key. Larchmont appeared on the monitor embedded in the wall behind him. His lips were moving but no words came out. "A hologram," Brisbane said. He glanced around. "I do the voiceover." He cleared his throat. "Would you like a sample?" he asked. The voice came from the image on the screen.

"How about Longstreet?" Brisbane offered.

Green waved him away from the console with his weapon. He walked over and surveyed the electronic gear. "What is it?" he said in puzzlement.

"The controlling computer," Brisbane exclaimed. "The whole kit and kaboodle." He saw the puzzlement on the faces around him. "That's an idiom."

"Apparently, so is security," Green muttered.

"Look," Brisbane said, "as long as you are here…I usually don't have much of an audience." He pressed two keys. Music filled the room. "What do you think?" he asked after giving them a few seconds to listen. "It's my newest composition."

"You're Mars' most famous composer," Townley said hesitantly. "I'm not sure any of us is qualified to judge…"

"I really would like an opinion," Brisbane said. "My father never liked my music. He was more of a traditionalist. You know, hip-hop, techno-rap and the like. I wanted something new, fresh." He glanced from face to face. "What do you think, Mr. Cantrell?" he asked Brown.

Brown shrugged. "I'm more into the classics, hip hop. This new stuff is really bad. It doesn't make my ears bleed. I also don't like to understand what the singer is saying," he said.

"My music has no lyrics," Brisbane said.

"Exactly," Brown replied.

"I like it," Green chimed in.

"Thanks," Brisbane said. "I'll just have to make some changes. The wood fife." He grimaced. "Well, you know. But I do have a saw." He touched the instrument on his desk. "And a gewgaw." He plucked at a small, key-shaped device with a string in the middle. "Plus, I do have lots of tapes. But that wood fife really helped."

"Enough," Brown thundered.

"Maybe we should pay him something for destroying the fife?" Mohr suggested. He looked at Green. "You shot it."

"I didn't know," Green mumbled. "I have only a few credits."

"How much does a fife cost?" Townley asked.

Brown glared at them. "We are trying to rescue political prisoners," he seethed, "not pay for fifes."

"Collateral damage," Kim suggested.

"A fife can cost one hundred to two hundred credits," Brisbane said. "You know there's no wood on Mars."

"That's it," Brown thundered. "We are just wasting time." He stared into Brisbane's face. "Where are the political prisoners kept?" he demanded.

"I don't know. I write music," Brisbane quavered. "Ask Townley. He's the tourist guide."

They all turned to look at Townley, who stepped back a few feet. He didn't know how to respond.

"I wouldn't believe anything he says," Brown snapped. "This place was supposed to be crawling with security."

"It usually is," Brisbane said hastily. Townley felt a sense of relief. Brisbane was covering for him. Maybe he did believe the kidnapping claim. "They have the afternoon off," the musician added.

"Androids?" Green asked.

"Oil and lube," Townley added hastily. "You know. Machines need service."

"You are so lucky," Brisbane said. "What great timing."

The computer beeped. Everyone looked at it. "For you?" Kim asked.

"We have to be careful," Townley threw in, hoping to help Brisbane. "Brisbane might seem like just a musician, but he wields great power here in Katarti. Isn't that right, Papa Bear?"

Puzzled for a moment, Brisbane caught on. "Yes," he said. "I suggest you leave before I notify the secret police." He gestured around the room. "As you can tell, there's no place to hide."

"We came to destroy that computer," Brown growled.

"This?" Brisbane gestured. "It's nothing. It creates the officials and leaves the rest to me to decide what's right."

"You really are Papa Bear," Townley gasped.

"Besides, there are four computers that work together. What you need is the master switch. That's in the base of the Judicial Center. Political prisoners are kept there, too."

"I thought you said you didn't know where the political prisoners were," Mohr challenged Brisbane.

"Oops," Brisbane said. "I wasn't supposed to tell anyone."

"The Judicial Center?" Green mused. "We have bombs planted there."

The Fakers looked at each other.

"Maybe we can use him as a hostage?" Kim thought aloud, pointing at Brisbane.

"I wouldn't recommend that," Townley said, trying to protect Brisbane. There was no reason both of them should be jeopardized. "I'm just as valuable."

"You don't need a hostage anyway," Brisbane added. "They just slow you down. Bad vibes."

"You got that right," Green said.

The computer beeped again. Brisbane leaned over and tapped several keys. He read the message. "You guys better get moving. The chief of security has just issued an order to arm the police with anti-alien lasers. They are far more powerful than those puny weapons you have."

"Geez," Mohr said. "I didn't even know there really are secret police."

"And you thought I was lying," Green said.

"How do we know there is a chief of security?" Green asked, waving at the computer. "Maybe it's just another avatar."

"Want to find out?" Brisbane asked. "Stick around." He looked at his watch. "It's almost time for the conjunction," he said.

"What!" Brown said.

"Another idiom," Mohr said. "We don't have much time."

"They must have spotted us coming out of that hole," Kim threw in.

"It took too long," Mohr added. Everyone looked at Brown who noticeably sucked in his stomach.

"It doesn't matter," Green said. "We can't change anything. "We've got to get outta here."

Brown grabbed Townley's arm. "Is there a back door?" he asked, glaring at the guide. Townley shook his head.

"Just an elevator," he managed. His arm ached.

"Sitting ducks," Brisbane said.

"Come on," Brown growled. He reached for Townley.

"Leave the guide," Brisbane suggested. Brown stopped. Townley looked back hopefully.

"We have his wife and son," Mohr said.

"Then you don't need him," Brisbane said. "He'll just get in the way."

"He's been pretty useless so far," Brown said.

"Absolutely," Townley agreed. "You are far better off without me."

The small group hesitated. "Hurry up," Brisbane said. "There's an army on its way."

The fivesome sped to the elevator. Brown waved his useless gun at Townley. "When we take over," he said as the elevator door opened, "you'll be the first to be exiled." In a moment, the elevator door closed.

Townley almost collapsed. He tottered to the desk and plopped down on the chair. He could barely read the message on the computer monitor: "Choir practice: four p.m."

CHAPTER 6

For a moment, Townley slumped in the chair. He could hear Brisbane doing something with the equipment, but didn't care. He felt completely exhausted. Finally, he managed to sit up. "Thank you," Townley mumbled at Brisbane.

The musician nodded and continued playing with some of the equipment on the wall. While relieved about escaping the terrorists, Townley kept studying the elevator. He half expected the doors to reopen and Brown or Green or someone to charge in to grab him. Instead, there was only silence.

Brisbane increased the music. It was atonal and anything but melodic, sort of a cross between a collision of a car and a building combined with animal sounds. Brisbane hummed along, glancing at Townley to see if he was reacting.

Townley heard the raucous noise, but didn't respond. He needed a few more minutes to recover. Running the past events through his head, he suddenly sat up and scrambled to pull his cell phone from his oversized pants.

"My god," he muttered.

"Is that good or bad?" Brisbane asked, thinking the guide was commenting on the music.

"My wife," Townley cried, hastily calling her.

"Hello, Cecil," she answered. "Must have been a long tour. How did it go?"

"Are you all right?" he gasped.

"Silly," Betsy replied. "I was just a little congested this morning. Little C is fine, too."

"You weren't kidnapped?" Townley tried.

"Have you been watching one of those dreadful police shows?" Betsy asked. "C and I have been at the park all morning, playing with some of his friends."

"Good," Townley mumbled, staring at the phone. Definitely Betsy's number and her voice. Didn't Mohr say the Fakers were holding her and C? Townley didn't know what to think anymore.

"We're having okra stew for supper," Betsy said. "I hope you'll be home soon." She paused. "What was that?"

Townley strained to hear something. "I don't know," he admitted.

"C," Betsy called urgently and hung up.

Townley lay back. "Now what?" he managed. He watched Brisbane for a moment, who was still improvising instruments and pausing to enter musical notes into his equipment. The audible sounds would change as he punched a key.

"More horned frog croaks?" the musician asked. "I also have a loon." He pressed another button.

No," Townley said, sitting up. He looked around the room, at the emptiness where there should have been something or some-one. Where were the monitors? Security? Where was any of the people he kept telling the tourists about? "What is going on?" Townley finally asked, addressing the open room as much as Brisbane.

"Listen to this," the musician said and stepped back from his wall unit. In a moment, various odd sounds combined to fill the room. Townley half heard the music.

Brisbane took the lack of response as non-approval. "Yeah," he said. "It's not very good. I wish I had that darn fife," he said. "It would give it a kind of deep tone. Maybe I can improvise." When Townley continued to look bewildered, Brisbane nodded. "I get it," he said. "Something different." He tapped the desk. "That's D sharp," he said. "I think." He ran to the paneled wall and patted it. "A flat," he decided. "Or B sharp." He looked at Townley. "What do you think?"

The guide shook his head. "I think I am going crazy," he said.

Larchmont appeared on the screen. "I prefer full orchestra-tion," he said. In a moment, he faded away.

Brisbane giggled. "I modeled him on my father," he announced.

"There are no security forces, are there?" Townley asked. He stood up. That had to be the answer. "No monitoring, no nothing."

"Sure there is," Brisbane said. "Everyone has been told over and over the security forces exist, so they do. No one does anything wrong because they have been told everything they do is being watched."

"But no one is," Townley said.

"Of course not," Brisbane replied. "Who wants to spend time watching everyone else?"

"The BIDs?" Townley asked.

Brisbane played some music, adding a drum beat to the final chords. "Just bracelets," he said.

"The cameras?"

"Dummies."

"Why?" Townley asked. All these years, every member of his family had guided newcomers and lied to all of them. He felt completely empty inside.

Brisbane played some more music. This time it was orchestral with some whale moans added for spice. Townley realized it was a selection from the Einstein. "Laarson was a genius," Brisbane said. "He wanted to make money and didn't want anything to upset the colony. He didn't have to spend on security. He only had to make people believe it existed."

"Oh," Townley moaned.

"He succeeded," Brisbane noted.

"Papa Bear?"

"That's what we called my great-grandfather," Brisbane said. "He was the first one to dispense with the old system. No one wanted to sit in boring council meetings. He had a hard time keeping automatons functioning there. They kind of dried up."

"My father never told me any of this," Townley mumbled. He began to walk around the room.

"No one was supposed to know," Brisbane said. "Life went on the same anyway."

"So no one was ever sent to Earth?"

"You like radiation?" Brisbane laughed using a Martian idiom. "You think folks on Earth would be happy if we kept dumping our miscreants on them? No, anyone misbehaving was told the next stop was Deadland. That cured a lot of folks really quick."

Somewhere, in the distance, they heard a boom. The building shook. Brisbane cocked an ear. "Ooh," he squealed. "E flat. That would be perfect for the third and fourth bars."

"Bombs," Townley said. That's what Betsy must have heard. They always had a bag packed for emergencies, such as a Mars quake or some other natural disaster. They all knew something could happen, even an asteroid the protective sheathing couldn't stop or an alien attack. Every resident was prepared to exit almost immediately. No doubt she was taking C to the entry tower.

"Is that sarcasm or do you really like it?" Brisbane asked.

Townley stood up. "I mean real bombs. The Fakers said they planted them all over," he said. "We have to get out of here."

Brisbane considered that. "Who would want to ruin Mars? No work. Lots of entertainment and activities. The weather never changes. It's downright perfect," he said.

Another blast shook the building.

"The Fakers have a different idea about perfection," Townley said. "How do we get the others out of here?" he asked Brisbane.

The musician tapped on the keys and stared at the computer monitor. It showed a line of people anxiously waiting at elevators to go through the observation deck to the surface. Behind them, plumes of red dust rose in the air. He clicked the keys. Rockets were standing in a row, waiting to leave as the people filed through tunnels leading to the ships. Townley hoped to see Betsy and his son, but everyone in line was totally hidden behind the protective shields.

"We can get all the residents evacuated in just a few hours," Brisbane said. "My great-grandfather arranged all that. He was the real Papa Bear. I would be Baby Bear, but the initials didn't work."

Townley's phone rang. "All aboard," Betsy reported.

"I'm coming," Townley said. The line went dead.

"Sad," Brisbane said. He tapped some keys. More music filled the air, this time with a martial sound. He gathered up his sheets of music and then realized there was no point. "Who will listen to my beautiful music on Earth," he said. "I'll be a nobody."

"No," Townley said, "you'll be a Martian."

CHAPTER 7

The elevator opened. Townley stepped in. No one was behind him. Brisbane had gone ahead. For some reason, Townley felt like he should be the last one to leave, sort of like the captain of a failing rocket. Brisbane may have been the latest Papa Bear, but he didn't give tours. He didn't know every inch of Mars.

Through the open door, Townley surveyed Katarti. The Caterpillar had stopped. Here and there, he spotted a few automatons still jerkily moving about amid the scattered rocks and crumpled buildings. Fed by unending electromagnetic waves, they could wander aimlessly for centuries. He could see the blue skies above. There, the white clouds were no longer moving. A network of small cracks now spread across the sky, like tiny lightning bolts embedded in the weakening concrete. Soon radiation, like rain, would begin falling on the doomed city. Bombs were still going off, echoing around the fallen walls and debris covered streets.

He imagined the Fakers were still searching for political prisoners and the nonexistent children used as imaginary sex slaves. They would still be here if new settlers ever return. He wondered if anyone would. Maybe some future Townley could serve as a tour guide.

The door closed. He continued to stare at it, refusing to look out the glass. He could hear the slight whirr of the engine as he rose up the long shaft to the observation platform. He told himself he could take one last look there, seeing the city from a distance might erase the obvious destruction. Up there, everything looked amazing and beautiful.

Stepping out onto the platform, he walked to the encircling glass overlooking Katarti. Blinking back tears, he realized a red haze covered the city, smothering the widespread destruction in a red blanket. He preferred to remember it that way.

Townley sighed. There was nothing left for him to do. No one to guide. Nothing to show anyone. He glanced to his left. The "welcome to Mars" sign was still on. The red lights seemed as bright. Even better, the sign was straight. *That was something*, Townley thought, pressing the elevator key for the final trip to the surface.

First impressions still mattered.

ABOUT THE AUTHOR

Born in Portland, Me., Bill Lazarus decided at a young age to be a writer. During his lengthy career in various media, he has won three international awards and was named Florida Feature Writer of the Year. Bill also taught writing at colleges and universities around the country. A nationally known religious historian, he has published more than 25 fiction and nonfiction books, including *Time Warp*, a three-part science fiction tale of revenge with a galaxy-hopping alien and his all-knowing, very cool, rocking horse. Bill and his wife live in Ormond Beach, Florida.

Other Books by
William Paul Lazarus

Time Warp: Book One

Forced to leave his own planet because of a civil war, Prince Anton flees into the unknown universe with only his all-knowing, automatonic horse, Thurgose, for company. En route to Earth, the closest inhabited planet, Anton quickly finds enemies are chasing him and he must veer to another planet where heralded fighters face off against weeds and poaching creates serious dangers. His space-ship damaged, he and Thurgose return to an Earth where every thought is captured by computers, as ambitious residents battle for the chance to get pills that will make them immortal. Trapped inside a military complex, Anton must find a way to escape, get back his ship, and somehow evade his enemies in the heavens above and on Earth. To do that, he has only a woman who has deserted her post to help him and an energy-deprived Thurgose.

Time Warp: Book Two

Trapped on Earth as his archenemy Wyron hovers dangerously in the sky above, Crown Prince Anton can only rely for assistance on his fantastic automatonic rocking horse Thurgose and a friendly bureaucrat named Bonnie. They try to hide with Outsiders, people who have rejected society's push for ratings to achieve immortality, finding Bonnie's brother among them. Wyron won't wait and attacks, forcing the Americans to turn to the only ones who can save them, Anton and Thurgose. With his ship repaired and joined by a human crew, Anton sets off for an epic battle.

Time Warp: Book Three

Two implacable enemies, Wyron and Dalian Crown Prince Anton, disagree on the fates of their respective planets, but must join forces when one spaceship is crippled in an interstellar battle. With two unexpected passengers, a mischievous hologram, a human crew and an all-purpose rocking horse named Thurgose, the two aliens head back to their own galaxy to discover what really happened. They must escape from pursuing Americans who are trying to rescue the humans on board, and overcome obstacles en route to Dalia. Moving rapidly by warping space, they move closer to finding the truth while discovering just how devious Thurgose can be.

More Books from
WolfSinger Publications

Cowboy Up – edited by Carol Hightshoe

Cowboy Up gathers stories that celebrate the timeless tradition of rodeo. The dust, the grit, the glory—it's all here.

From the echoes of the past to the rodeo arenas of today, these stories will take you on a wild ride through the highs and lows of rodeo life. You'll share in their triumphs and their heartbreaks. From the unbreakable bond between rider and horse to the courage it takes to get back in the saddle after a fall, this anthology is a tribute to the spirit that keeps rodeo alive.

But this book isn't just about telling stories. It's about giving back. Eighty-Five percent of proceeds from Cowboy Up will be donated to the Justin Cowboy Crisis Fund, a non-profit organization dedicated to helping injured rodeo athletes get back on their feet. Your purchase helps support those who risk it all in the arena, offering them a lifeline when they need it most.

So saddle up. Dive into these tales of resilience, heart, and the cowboy way. With every story, you're not just reading about rodeo —you're helping to keep its spirit alive.

Homefall Search – Dana Bell

Charged with finding the best place for a new Homefall, Jehna Talon searched on Saris, a world located in the Tashiti Nebula. Along with her Arial shapeshifter companions, she goes into the Ghost Mountains to find a specific valley, only to become trapped during a storm and encounters a native dragon.

With local rancher Harrison Talbot she negotiates the price for the land. Brides, for him and his hands. As her uncle taught her, there's always a need to be filled. Traveling to Aris and with the help of a local contact, she finds women willing to brave the frontiers of space.

Returning to Ronia, home of the Talons, she learns opposition from the other clan leaders may stop the dream she had of becoming a clan leader. They argue there are too few Rovers and she'll never succeed.

Could they be right, despite her already finding the ideal location?

The Dragon's Hoard 3 – edited by Carol Hightshoe

In this anthology, twenty-six authors weave enchanting stories of dragons—from the fierce and fire-breathing to the wise and benevolent. Enter a treasure trove of tales where dragons reign supreme and hoards are more than mere gold.

Discover hidden gems of wisdom and magic within these lairs. Feast on tales that shimmer with magic, adventure, and the timeless allure of dragons. Explore the myriad treasures dragons hold dear and the legends that surround them.

From heartwarming tales of friendship and loyalty to thrilling adventures filled with danger and magic, these tales offer something for every dragon lover. Whether they are guardians of treasure, seekers of knowledge, or forces of nature: the dragons in this collection will ignite your imagination.

The Dragon's Hoard 2 – edited by Carol Hightshoe

Welcome to realms where dragons reign, treasures abound, and every adventure leads to magic. Explore stories that spark the imagination and might just awaken the dragon within. Are you brave enough to face the dragon and claim your prize?

From the unyielding grip of ancient magics to the cunning of those who seek dragons, their treasure or both—each story weaves a rich tapestry of magic and lore.

Whether it's a battle for survival, the forging of an unlikely alliance, or a humorous twist on hoarding habits, our authors invite you to delve into realms where dragons not only hoard gold but also secrets, spells, and sometimes, even friendships. After all, in the world of dragons, not all treasures are silver and gold—some are stories waiting to be told.

The Hounds of Ardagh – Laura J Underwood

Ginny Ni Cooley never desired more than the simple life she had, living in Tamhasg Wood and using her magic to occasionally assist the folk of Conorscroft while putting up with the machinations of the ghost of her former mentor Manus MacGreeley. But her peace is shattered one night with the arrival of a lad who is fleeing a pack of red-gold hounds led by a hound-shaped demon known as Nidubh.

So much for peace and solitude. By rescuing Fafne MacArdagh, Ginny becomes wrapped in the fabric of an intrigue involving a family feud, a traitorous son, and a blood mage named Edain who is determined to keep her soul. It is she who cast a spell on Fafne's family and household and transformed the MacArdaghs into hounds.

Ginny gives Fafne her word to take him to Caer Keltora so they can report the matter to the Council of Mageborn. But Edain is determined to keep her secret and her soul intact and moves to thwart Ginny at every turn.

For Ginny Ni Cooley who has faced many bogies, dealing with a demon, a bloodmage and the Dark Lord of Annwn will be no easy task. But she will do what she must to undo Edain's spells. If not, Manus' soul will become part of Arawn's Cauldron of Doom. Ginny will become a demon's feast, and poor Fafne will join the Hounds of Ardagh.

Wee Folk and Wise: A Fairies Anthology
– edited by Deby Fredericks

All over the world, fairy tales are told.
There are big fairies and little fairies.
Ugly fairies and pretty fairies.
Wise fairies and silly fairies.
Sweet fairies and scary fairies.

Seventeen authors share their own fantastic fairy tales in this magical collection. What kind of fairy will you meet here?

Infinity – Ted Pennella

In the distant future, when peace between humanity and the artificial intelligences their ancestors created has been settled, Conrad Conner tries to live a quiet and unassuming life in orbit about Jupiter on the city-station Socrates' Odyssey. When Conner's attempt to create a prototypical communication artificial for use by the Sol-Humana Confederation's Stellar Fleet gets derailed by the attempted murder of the very artificial he's created, his life spirals into a mad flight back to Earth to try and save at least his sister's children, if not his sister herself. Past failures and heartaches resurface as seemingly unconnected dots become a plot by the First Admiral to steal not just power over the Confederation, but a secret Conner holds within himself.

A secret not even Conner knows about.

Flatlanders - Mike Sherer

Young theoretical physicist Mickey Haiku has fallen into Eden's trap. She is a much smarter scientist who is intent on saving her own dimension by destroying his. Unbeknownst to either, beings from several yet higher dimensions have their own strategies. This sends the mixed-up pawns off on a wild odyssey through a dozen weird, twisted dimensions. As if this hyper-dimensional odyssey isn't challenging enough for Mickey, he has the additional difficulty of embarking on this whacko tour as a (pregnant!) female. Which means Eden is stuck in Mickey's body. The two are soon forced to cooperate since each holds the other's body hostage.

The strangest relationship this side of the 11th dimension develops between the two.

Fires of Rapiveshta: Book Three: A Familiar's Tale
– Verna Mckinnon

With Obsydia's chaos growing and more kingdoms falling under her control, Runa, Mellypip and their friends scramble to find a way to stop her from discarding her mortal form and claiming their world in the name of her Eternal Father Ahridum and plunging it into a never-ending age of darkness and evil.

The dragons of Rapiveshta are awakened from their long slumber by Obsydia's attempt to steal the egg that holds the unborn dragon who will become the next leader of the dragon clans. The egg is given to Runa's grandfather to protect it. When it hatches, Mellypip finds himself bonded to the baby dragon as her guardian.

As Obsydia reaches the climax of the ritual that will burn away her mortality, Runa, Opaline and Panthara find themselves captured to be used as sacrifices. Will the Gate of Souls claim Runa and Mellypip as the Winged Fey have foreseen? Or will the Fires of

Rapiveshta and those chosen to be the Scions of Light be able to save them and their world.

Borne in the Blood – edited by Carol Hightshoe

Delve into the mysterious and powerful world of blood in "Borne in the Blood"

This collection of enthralling stories explores the multifaceted essence of blood—as a symbol of life, a medium of magic, and a bond of kinship. From the chilling tale of a minstrel haunted by a spectral king to the whimsical account of a vampire ice cream vendor, each story weaves a unique narrative around the theme of blood. Encounter a woman whose body bizarrely intertwines with metallic elements, and follow a girl's journey as she confronts her isolation due to her heritage. Feel chills as those who were wronged reach across the years to have their final revenge on the blood descendants of those who oppressed them.

Shifters, Vampires, Witches, and other ordinary and extraordinary folk—all bound together by that which they carry in their blood.

These tales will transport you through a spectrum of emotions, from the depths of fear to the heights of fantasy, as you unravel the mysteries and power that lie within the blood.

Proceeds from sales of Borne in the Blood will be donated to the Multiple Myeloma Research Foundation – themmrf.org/

And more – check out our books at
www.wolfsingerpubs.com

www.ingramcontent.com/pod-product-compliance
Lightning Source LLC
Chambersburg PA
CBHW072029170626
46811CB00008B/3001